"Where have I been?"

"That's right. Answer me, and be quick about it," Flynn Parker snapped. "I want to know where you've been for the past two years."

Irritation began to break through Annie's stunned amazement. "Right here on the island—"

"The devil you were. Two years and three months ago you were in Seattle."

Her arms crossed defensively over her stomach. "How do you know that? Did we meet there?"

"You're trying to tell me you don't remember how we met?"

"I don't remember you at all."

"Well, it's unfortunate that you don't, since I'm your husband."

Dear Reader,

Help us celebrate life, love and happy-ever-afters with our great new series.

Everybody loves a party, and birthday parties best of all, so join some of your favorite authors and celebrate in style with seven fantastic new romances. One for every day of the week, in fact, and each featuring a truly wonderful woman whose story fits the lines of the old rhyme, "Monday's child is..."

> Monday's child is fair of face,
> Tuesday's child is full of grace,
> Wednesday's child is full of woe,
> Thursday's child has far to go,
> Friday's child is loving and giving,
> Saturday's child works hard for its living.
> And a child that's born on a Sunday
> Is bonny and blithe and good and gay.

(Anon.)

Does the day on which you're born affect your character? Some people think so—if you want to find out more read our exciting new series. Available wherever Harlequin books are sold:

May	#3407	*The Marriage Business*	Jessica Steele
June	#3412	*Private Dancer*	Eva Rutland
July	#3417	*Coming Home*	Patricia Wilson
August	#3422	*Desperately Seeking Annie*	Patricia Knoll
September	#3424	*A Simple Texas Wedding*	Ruth Jean Dale
October	#3429	*Working Girl*	Jessica Hart
November	#3434	*Dream Wedding*	Helen Brooks

Happy reading,

The Editors, Harlequin Romance

Desperately
Seeking Annie
Patricia Knoll

Harlequin Books

TORONTO • NEW YORK • LONDON
AMSTERDAM • PARIS • SYDNEY • HAMBURG
STOCKHOLM • ATHENS • TOKYO • MILAN
MADRID • WARSAW • BUDAPEST • AUCKLAND

For my aunt and uncle, Opal and Harlon Green—
because they tell family stories I love to hear.

ISBN 0-373-03422-9

DESPERATELY SEEKING ANNIE

First North American Publication 1996.

CHAPTER ONE

"DON'T scowl at them like that, Flynn. I don't think you realize it, but your scowls scare the daylights out of people."

Flynn Parker paused in his pacing and frowned at his younger sister, Brenna. "What?"

She burst out laughing. "See? There you go again. You look like you could bite iron nails in half."

"Why can't they hurry?" he groused, crossing the terminal of the small regional airport in Santa Barbara County to gaze at the mechanic and pilot who were attempting to repair a minor problem on the plane that was to take him to Anapamua Island.

Brenna rose lazily to her feet and ambled across to stand beside him. She hooked her arm in his, an easy task since she was nearly as tall as he was. Tilting her head, she gave him a look full of love and humored exasperation. "They can't hurry because every time they start making some progress, you either stomp out there to ask what the holdup is, or you stand here and glare at them. They're so nervous they keep dropping their tools. That pilot has probably flown combat missions that were easier than coming in here to tell you that the flight was delayed."

"Don't be ridiculous." Flynn snorted. "I don't make people nervous."

"Are you kidding? Mother and I received petitions from every hotel in the Parker chain begging us to send you on a vacation, but as far away from them as possible."

"Very funny." Flynn looked at his sister as a reluctant smile edged his mouth. "*You're* the only person who would have nerve enough to write up a petition like that."

"And thank heaven, I don't work for you." Blond and willowy, with a sassy grin and a sense of humor to match, Brenna was exactly the opposite of everyone else in their family. Flynn knew he and his father had always worked too hard, approached everything far too seriously. Their mother was a quiet woman, organized and intense. The three of them had been taken totally by surprise when Brenna arrived shortly after Flynn's tenth birthday. She had shaken up their private world, and Flynn, for one, had been eternally grateful. He couldn't even imagine what kind of workaholics the three of them would have become without her.

She was easygoing and fun, liked most people she met and accepted them at face value. She was in her last year of veterinarian's school, and Flynn was fiercely proud of her. She had insisted on flying from San Francisco with him to make sure he really left on his vacation and didn't detour by one of his own hotels to do a few days' work.

As she watched him, Brenna's dark eyes clouded and she reached up to dust an imaginary speck from his lapel. "You will try to relax, won't you? You won't spend too much time brooding, or worse yet, working?" She directed an irritated look at the briefcase by the door. "That thing had better not hold anything more than a spare toothbrush."

"I have to do some work, but I've already promised not to do too much, haven't I?"

"And you always keep your promises. I'm counting on that." She paused, took a deep breath and said, "You made me another promise, remember?"

Flynn lifted his chin and looked away from her. Her sunny nature tugged at him, trying to pull him out of the place where he had locked away his deepest emotions.

He gazed out the window but saw only his own reflection. Brenna was right. His scowl was formidable. It only served to add darkness to his face, already accented by black hair and deep green eyes beneath thick brows. He nodded. "I remember."

"It's been two years, and if you haven't heard anything in that time...if she's made no attempt at all to contact you..."

"I know," he cut her off impatiently, not wanting to be reminded.

Unoffended, Brenna went up on her tiptoes to give him a hug. "It's time for you to get on with your life."

Flynn softened. After all, it wasn't her fault that he'd let a woman make a fool of him. He returned the hug. "So you keep telling me."

Brenna sighed and shook her head. "But you make your own decisions. Always have. Always will."

"I'm the one who has to live with them."

"And Mother and I have to live with you, not a pleasant task lately. I hope this vacation helps."

"It will. I'll make a decision one way or the other while I'm away."

"Good." Satisfied, she gave him another squeeze as the pilot came through the door to say that the plane was ready for takeoff.

Flynn kissed Brenna goodbye and strode to the small twin-engine plane. As he strapped himself in, he wished again that he could have flown in the Parker Hotel company jet, but it was in for its regular maintenance check and he had been too impatient and restless to wait for it. The only consolation was that he was the sole passenger on this little twin-engine craft. He wouldn't be expected to indulge in idle chatter, a pastime he loathed anyway.

They were soon airborne, and within half an hour, the clouds split and mist evaporated as the aircraft dipped one wing and banked to circle Anapamua, the last link in the chain that made up California's Channel Islands. Small and rocky, with only one small stand of pine forest and acres of chaparral, it looked like an isolated jewel in the dark jade setting of the Pacific Ocean. Santa Barbara, twenty-five miles east, might have been in another galaxy.

Flynn looked out at the stark beauty of the island, his attention focused on his destination, the three-story brick building known as the Anapamua Island Inn. Besides the twenty-room hotel, the island also had a nine-hole golf course, hiking paths, tennis courts, a cove sheltered enough for swimming and a boat dock where a small cabin cruiser bobbed lazily on the waves. Many guests came by boat from the city, and in good weather, fishing boats from Santa Barbara stopped by to pick up customers for a day of deep-sea fishing. The location was perfect and the facilities looked well kept. From all he had heard, the place was efficiently run by a small staff headed by one of the owners. He would see for himself how well it was run. His interest was personal as well as professional. He wished he hadn't been delayed.

Sighing, he gave himself a mental shake. Speed wasn't important today, or for the next couple of weeks. He was on vacation, the first one he'd had in two years and, as Brenna had already reminded him, he was supposed to relax. Fishing, tennis, long hours spent in the sun slathered with sunscreen, those were the orders of his mother and sister who were worried that he'd been working too hard.

They were right, of course. He always worked too hard, even more so since his father had died and he had taken over the company. He didn't know any other way to live. If hard work could drive out demons, his should have been long gone, but they weren't. He had to learn to relax, and that's why he'd come to beautiful, lonely Anapamua. At least, it was one of the reasons.

Flynn leaned closer to the window as the plane banked once again and headed for the little landing strip at the end of the island. To reach it, they flew over the gardens of the inn, squares of carefully tended emerald in the gray-green chaparral.

In one section, a woman straightened and pushed her long, strawberry-blond hair out of her eyes. She looked up as though startled, lifting her hand defensively to shield her face. After a moment's pause, her hand opened and she waved in a friendly way, welcoming the plane. Flynn gripped the armrest and snapped to attention, his head swinging around just as the aircraft passed over her and she disappeared beneath the wing.

Damn, he thought, leaning his head back and closing his eyes. When was he going to stop looking for what he knew he would never again see? For too long now, every woman with hair the color of a sunset had caught his eye. None of them had ever been the one he sought. It was still happening and it had to stop.

He knew he had a possessive personality, bordering on obsessive. It was one of the things that made him successful. He never let go of anything until it was arranged to his satisfaction. Maybe Brenna was right, though. Maybe it was time for him to let go of the past. It was possible that this one thing could not be resolved the way he wanted it. He would give it more thought on this vacation and come to a final decision. It was time.

Annie Locke hurriedly finished gathering her pruning shears and the basket she had filled with yellow marguerite daisies and fronds from her favorite shrub, the breath of heaven. She ran a trembling hand over the branches and watched the supple movement as they swayed in the wind, then settled into stillness.

With them, the pace of her heart slowed and the shaking stopped. She swallowed the lump of terror that had formed in her throat and blinked away the tears that had rushed into her deep blue eyes. It was getting easier, she realized with hard-won satisfaction. The plane, so much like the one on which her parents had died, no longer filled her with sick panic. She certainly wasn't ready to fly again herself, but at least she could now look at an airplane without shuddering with horror.

She smoothed her waist-length red-gold hair away from her face and caught it at the side of her head with one hand to keep the blowing strands from her eyes as she stepped through the garden gate and closed it behind her. With a relieved sigh, she began walking toward the hotel. She was a small woman, and the force of the wind urged her along the path. The wide legs of her loose gabardine trousers billowed around her.

Seeing the aircraft always bothered her, and she usually tried to be inside when she knew it was coming in. She wasn't avoiding seeing it, she had convinced herself. She was merely easing herself back into daily contact. Up until a few months ago, even visual contact had been more than she could bear.

Annie was grateful for the flights Gary Mendoza's charter service made to Anapamua. He brought many of their guests, and today he was bringing a very special one, the one for whose room she was personally picking her favorite flowers. The groundskeeper, Martin, waiting at the airstrip with the hotel's Jeep, would pick up their guest and deliver him to the front entrance. If she hurried, she could be there to greet him, but it might be better if she didn't seem overanxious—even though she was.

It was still weeks before the beginning of the regular vacation season, and they were just finishing a particularly wet and gloomy winter and spring. The inn needed all the guests it could get if she hoped to operate in the black this year.

They were even being blessed with a rare day of good weather in honor of his arrival. Annie strolled along swinging her basket and gazing at the inn.

Built in the twenties as a weekend getaway for a Hollywood silent film star who had possessed more money than common sense, the Tudor-style building looked wildly out of place on the wind-swept island. It had wood-shingle walls above the native fieldstone of the first floor and diamond-paned casement windows that were a challenge to keep polished.

No expense had been spared on the inside. The floors and trim were of mahogany, as was the elaborately carved staircase to the second and third floors. All decorating had been done in the grand style of the Roaring Twenties and had eaten up the film star's life savings. By the time the stock market crashed in 1929, he had been flat broke and willing to sell the place to Annie's grandfather for a fraction of its worth.

Annie was glad that her grandfather had bought the mansion and turned it into an inn. She loved it with deep passion. If she ever married, it would be to a man who would be willing to live and work at the inn. She never intended to leave again. She smiled ruefully. That plan, of course, had greatly limited the number of suitors she'd had.

As she neared the service entrance, Annie spied a small, forlorn figure seated on the back step, bouncing a soccer ball between his feet. She fought a grin as he looked up hopefully then dropped his chin against his chest.

"Hi, Luis. What's the matter?"

"Nobody to play with," he grumbled. "Just old people around."

Annie swallowed a laugh. The middle-aged and retired vacationers currently staying at the inn might take exception to Luis's eight-year-old view. There were usually children staying at the inn for him to play with once he had finished his daily lessons. His mother, Beatrice, was the head housekeeper and sometimes she helped out at the front desk. His father, Carlos, was the inn's maintenance man. They home-schooled him and would board him with a family in the city when it came time for high school. Annie had done the same thing but had hated being away from the island. Luis was a bold, adventurous little boy. She knew he would love living and going to school in the city.

She gathered her full trousers around her and joined him on the step, placing the flowers atop her knees. Arranging them could wait a few minutes.

"I've noticed you're getting pretty good at this game."

Luis sent her a pleased look, then sighed. "I'd be better if I had someone to practice with."

She laid the flowers aside. "Would a girl do?"

"Girls can't play soccer."

She rolled her eyes and tugged on his ear. "Oh, no, a budding chauvinist. There are girls' soccer teams all over the world."

He ducked away from her. "A butting what?"

"Never mind." She stood briskly. "This girl can play soccer. Come on."

Luis gave her a doubtful look, but he scrambled to his feet and the two of them engaged in a rousing ten-minute game that took them around the side of the building.

Annie knew that such behavior probably wasn't proper for an innkeeper, but in her opinion, the happiness of one small boy was more important than dignity.

They had decided that the goal would be the area between two juniper bushes. Annie tried to block the ball, but Luis scored a goal, then whooped in triumph. Annie swept him into a congratulatory hug which he returned before he wiggled away and grinned. "You're pretty good—for a girl."

She flung her arms wide as she laughed. "So are you—for a boy."

He scooped up the ball. "Come on. I want to tell my dad that I beat you."

She turned toward the service entrance, but as they passed beneath the windows, Annie thought she saw movement at one of them. She glanced up, but Luis tugged her around the corner.

She was sure the movement had been at Mr Parker's window. With a sigh, she decided she had better show a little more restraint.

While Luis ran to find his father, Annie headed for the kitchen.

*   *   *

Flynn flipped back the lacy curtain and cranked open the casement window. Quickly, he scanned the lawn just in time to see a flash of red-gold disappear around the corner. It was the same woman. He'd heard her laugh and the carefree sound had drawn him to the window.

Flynn moved his shoulders in a restless movement, puzzled by his uncharacteristic reaction. He felt as if a hot electrical wire had flicked across his skin, touching a raw nerve.

Flynn frowned, not liking the sensation at all. He couldn't imagine why he was reacting like this to a woman's laugh, except that he'd never before heard anything like it. The sound was like water tumbling over pebbles, rising and falling in a rush. It was so warm and inviting that he wanted to reach out and grab it—if one could grab a sound.

Something about it made him think of the future, of the dark, empty days and years ahead of him. It was time he would face alone unless he made the decision to close out the past two years of his life and move ahead.

He let the curtain fall into place as he turned to the room. He glanced around, approving the homelike atmosphere and the comfortable though worn furnishings. He set his briefcase on the desk and removed a laptop computer. Despite what he had promised Brenna, he had to get *some* work done. He began punching the keys and within moments was engrossed in his task.

At the kitchen entrance, Annie wiped her feet, then pushed her way inside. Immediately, the cook,

Mary Fredericks, turned from where she was rolling pie dough and gave her a sharp look.

"What have you been doing?"

Annie gave her an unrepentant grin. "Playing soccer with Luis." She held up her hand as if to ward off a storm. "Don't worry. I wiped my feet."

"Good. I think Mr Parker's arrived," Mary said, returning to her work. She rolled, fitted and trimmed the dough into the pie tins with amazing speed, then cut tiny leaf shapes to decorate the edges of the top crust.

Annie's mother had always said the inn couldn't have run without Mary. She had arrived more than twenty-five years ago, suitcase in hand and small son in tow, widowed by the war in Vietnam and looking for a way to support herself and her boy. She looked hardly older now than she had then, though Annie had begun to notice a few streaks of gray in her light brown hair.

Watching her work had always been one of Annie's favorite pastimes, although she admitted that having Mary around was the reason she never learned to cook. She helped out with some of the simpler tasks and the washing up, but had never made a meal on her own. Why bother when she lived in the same hotel as one of the world's best chefs?

"Did you see him?" Annie asked as she carried the flowers and a couple of vases to the large utility sink across the room. She began trimming the leaves and stems and arranging the blossoms carefully.

"No, I've got too much to do to hang around the front desk. Martin checked him in."

Annie groaned in dismay. "I thought Beatrice was going to be at the desk."

"She was, but Mrs Grindle wasn't satisfied with the way the fire was laid in her room. Beatrice went to see about it. She'll be gone for a while, because Mrs Shaw and Mrs Bennett will want theirs laid exactly like their sister's."

"Whoever invented the saying, 'The customer is always right,' had never met those three." The women were sisters, middle-aged identical triplets who had visited the inn every spring for as long as she could remember for what they called Sister's Week. Annie loved having repeat guests and these three had recommended many people to the inn, but they were engaged in a lifelong game of keeping up with sister that nearly drove the staff crazy. Whatever one of them had, the others wanted, and they were all three hard to please.

"Thank goodness they only stay for a week and they leave great tips for everyone," Mary added.

Annie laughed, then returned to the subject uppermost in her mind. "I hope Martin remembered to wash his hands before checking Mr Parker in." Martin was fresh out of high school, an excellent gardener and eager to learn all he could from Carlos, but definitely lacking in sanitary standards. "James is still sick?" James was Mary's son, recently discharged from the Marines and working at the inn until he could begin college classes in the fall. He was Annie's best friend and she had missed him terribly while he had been in the military.

"Sick as a kid tasting his first cigarette," Mary said. "I don't know where he picked up this flu bug but it's a bad one."

"Probably one of the guests brought it in." Annie finished arranging the flowers and held up the vase. "There. How's that?"

Mary eyed it critically. "Take out some of the greenery. You're drowning the flowers. I suppose you're going to deliver those personally."

"Certainly."

"Parker might think you're trying too hard."

"I *am* trying too hard." Annie plucked out some of the breath of heaven. "Why do you think he's really here?"

"For a vacation." Mary slid her pies into the oven and closed the door carefully.

"Why would a man who owns some of the nicest hotels in the world want to stay at an out-of-the-way place like this island?"

"Probably because it *is* out of the way. If he went to one of his own hotels, the staff would be on pins and needles trying to make him comfortable and probably driving him crazy. I've heard he's not the most patient man in the world, doesn't suffer fools gladly and can't stand fawning."

"I've heard the same thing." Satisfied with her arrangements at last, Annie picked up the two vases and held them up to receive Mary's nod of approval. "I guess you're right. He probably just wants time alone. Running a major hotel chain can't be easy, especially since he took it over when he was barely thirty."

Mary's brows lifted and she rested her flour-dusted hands against her waist. "I didn't know you knew so much about him."

Annie gave her friend a swift look. Mary knew her too well and saw too much. Annie herself didn't know why he interested her so. As far as she could recall, she had never even seen a photograph of him. Interviews with him focused on his hotels, as did all the accompanying pictures.

She shrugged. "I've read about him." Anxious to halt any more questions from Mary, she hurried for the swinging door that connected the kitchen to the dining room. "I'll be right back to help with dinner."

She had found the information about Flynn Parker to be fascinating reading. His father, the founder of Parker Hotels, had died about the same time her own parents had, and she sympathized with Flynn. Immediately after taking over the hotels, he had been forced to fight off a takeover bid from rival hotels. Since then, he had worked ceaselessly to ensure the success of the chain and the happiness of the stockholders.

Flynn Parker was the wonder boy of the industry just now, having come up with innovative ideas for families to afford vacations together. He also gave one free night's lodging in the honeymoon suites of each of his hotels to newlyweds who presented proof of their marriage upon check-in and stayed at least one more night at their own expense. People in the industry had laughed at that tactic, but it had proven to be so successful that it wasn't long before they were copying his methods.

Even Annie had considered it until she realized that due to the harsh winter and late arrival of spring, the inn was already losing money. She couldn't afford to give away free lodging just now. Things would be better soon. A beautiful, clear summer was expected, and they had been receiving calls to book reservations.

She passed through the dining room, automatically checking to see that the tables had been set for dinner. She and Beatrice and one full-time waitress handled the serving of the guests, though lately there hadn't been much of a crowd.

The inn had an elevator, the old-fashioned kind with a folding metal grille for a door, but she took the stairs to the second floor, carrying the two vases carefully.

When she reached the door of the best suite, she set the flowers on a hall table and checked her appearance in the mirror above it, running a hand over her hair to smooth it and straightening the collar of her yellow print blouse.

Satisfied, she knocked on the door of the suite and waited for an answer.

"Come on in," a masculine voice called out. "I'm on the phone."

Annie tilted her head curiously. Was there something familiar about his voice? Shaking her head, she used her passkey to enter. She expected to see her guest, but the sitting room was empty. The bedroom door stood ajar and she could hear him speaking. She closed the door to the suite, then looked around, startled at the changes that must have taken place in less than half an hour.

Flynn Parker certainly made space for himself.

A small writing desk near the window had been cleared of its blotter, container of pens and leather folder of hotel stationery. In their place was an impressive laptop computer, already switched on. The sheer draperies over the windows had been looped back to let in light and the casement window cranked outward to catch the breeze. It *must* have been him at the window. Her cheeks flushed at the memory. She noticed that the coffee table had been moved to one end of the Queen Anne style sofa to widen the floor area. A handful of change, a set of keys and a pearl-handled penknife were heaped in an ashtray.

An odd feeling of familiarity touched her again, sending tingling awareness skidding across her shoulders. She shivered. The feeling wasn't new. She'd felt it many times, more lately than before. She told herself it meant nothing.

When she heard the bedroom phone being dropped onto its cradle, she cleared her throat and called out, "Mr Parker, welcome to Anapamua Island Inn. I've brought some flowers." She set one vase on top of the displaced coffee table and the other on the credenza that held the entertainment center. "I'm glad to see you're making yourself comfortable. Please let me know if you need anything. I'll be glad to take care of it personally."

"What the...?"

Annie was jolted when the bedroom door was slammed back against the wall. She whirled around to see a tall man with midnight-black hair and intense green eyes rush into the room. With a squeak, she stumbled backward as he came to a stop a few feet from her.

Her hand flew to her throat. "Mr Parker, you startled me," she gasped, fighting for her lost breath. Why was he staring at her like that. As if he had seen a ghost?

He didn't answer for a few seconds. His eyes searched her face, swept over her and searched her face again. His mouth worked as if it was having a hard time forming words, and finally he spoke in a low, fierce voice. "What the devil are you doing here?"

"I knocked and you said I could come in..." Her words of explanation dried up as he continued to stare at her. She couldn't understand what was wrong with him, and the force of his astounded expression had her words lurching over each other. Helplessly, she pointed to the vases. "I...I was...I brought you some flowers... I thought you might like..."

"Where have you been?"

Her hands dropped to her sides. "Where have I been?"

"That's right. Answer me and be damned quick about it."

Nothing she had read or heard had suggested that the head of Parker Hotels was crazy. How could the journalists who had interviewed him have missed such an important fact? Maybe he was upset because he had expected her to meet him personally at the front desk.

"I was outside," she said, slowly and carefully. "I picked some flowers for your room. I'm sorry

I didn't meet you when you arrived, but I was sure the staff could handle your check in...."

"I don't give a damn about check in," he snapped. "I want to know where the devil you've been for the past two years."

She gaped at him. "Why on earth would you want to know that?"

"Quit stalling! Answer me."

Irritation began to break through her stunned amazement. Her arms flew wide to encompass the room and the world outside. "Right here on this island where I've lived all my life."

"The devil you were. Two years and three months ago you were in Seattle."

Annie's heart began pounding in her throat and the beat spread until it shook her whole body. Her arms crossed defensively over her stomach. "How do you know that? Did we meet there?"

His mouth pulled into a flat, harsh line. "You're trying to tell me you don't remember how we met?"

She jerked her head once, in a quick, sharp negative. "I don't remember you at all."

His head jutted forward and his hands rose to his waist. "Well, it's unfortunate that you don't since I'm your husband."

CHAPTER TWO

ANNIE'S first instinct was to laugh, but the fierceness in his expression killed the bubble of hysteria that rose in her throat. "My husband?"

"Yes, *your* husband."

She shook her head so vigorously her hair flew around her in a cloud. Compelled by self-preservation, her feet moved back a step, putting a protective distance between them. "No. I've never been married."

"What kind of game is this?"

"You've got me mixed up with someone else."

His sharp gaze made another quick catalog of her features, but this time, they burned with dismissive anger. "Strawberry-blond hair, dark blue eyes, small scar on the back of your left elbow..."

Annie gasped and her hand flew automatically to hide the spot, although it was covered by the long sleeve of her blouse. "How... how did you know about that?"

He ignored her question as he continued relentlessly. He loomed over her and she watched angry color shifting in his eyes, from dark green to almost black. "No, Anne Christina Locke, I don't have you mixed up with someone else. I know exactly who you are, and you know who I am. If you didn't want me after only six weeks, why didn't you just say so? I would have given you a divorce, though probably not a settlement," he added in a cruel tone. "You weren't around long enough for me to find out if you were worth a settlement."

Annie held her hands out, palms up. Her breath squeezed from her lungs in a dry wheeze. "I don't know what you're talking about." She tried to run her tongue across her dry lips, but she could only stand and stare at him. "This...this is a joke, right? Someone put you up to this. James, maybe, he's always been quite a—"

"Stop it!" Flynn drew in a sharp breath. "Stop it. Don't bother pretending you don't remember me."

"I *don't*."

"You don't remember marrying me on February third two years ago?"

"No."

"You don't remember moving into my apartment on the top floor of the Parker Hotel Seattle and the time we lived there together?"

"Of course not," she shot back. "How could I? It never happened! I...I couldn't have forgotten that..." Something was choking off her air. Fright, panic, maybe her own heart. The edges of her vision began to blacken. Annie gasped and tried to draw oxygen into her lungs. She lurched away from him, heading blindly for the door. "I've got to get out of here."

She hadn't gone two steps before he caught her arm, his fingers like shackles on her flesh. "You're not running again."

Annie tried to wrench from his grasp. "I've got to get some air."

"Come over by the window." He half dragged her there, shoving the writing desk out of the way so she could have access to the breeze.

Dizzily, Annie leaned against the cool wood of the frame, closed her eyes and tried to breathe deeply.

This was frightening—horrifying. She wanted to run from him, to dash downstairs and have Carlos and Martin drag this crazy man away, but they probably couldn't handle him, and she couldn't move. Waves of nausea washed over her, making her too weak to run.

Flynn Parker stood behind her, blocking her escape. She wondered if he was afraid to let her leave the room, thinking she might leave the island. But the cabin cruiser was too slow for her to flee from him, and she didn't fly. He didn't know that, though, because he didn't know her, not really, or he wouldn't be suffering this delusion that they'd been married. Married! Despite the gap in her memory, she would know if she'd ever been married.

Shakily, she opened her eyes, and slowly, reluctantly turned her head to look at him. His face was ashen, his eyes dark with anger and shock strong enough to match her own. She almost felt sorry for him until he spoke in a tone that dripped ice chips. "That's enough theatrics. Why the fainting act? Did you think I'd never find you?"

Anger gave her strength to push away from him and step backward into the room. "It's not an act. How could I care one way or another if you found me, since I don't know you except by reputation and have no idea what you're talking about?" With trembling hands, she pushed her hair behind her shoulders, then she straightened and faced him. "Tell me what makes you think we're married."

His powerful hands formed fists at his sides. "It's not a matter of thinking, it's a matter of knowing— just as you know."

"No," she said with wild desperation. "Don't you understand? I've told you I don't—"

"Cut it out," he snapped in a savage tone. "Stop pretending. What do you hope to gain by it? You can't have forgotten that we were married."

"But I *have*." Her voice was a strangled cry. "If...if it's true." In spite of being near the window, she felt that she was choking with panic. "If it's true that we were, and I'm not saying it is, I don't remember it."

"Sure you don't," he snorted. Flynn seemed to be recovering from his shock much more rapidly than she was. Color was returning to his face, but his eyes were murderous.

"Was it for money?" he asked. "Another man? I never heard about one, but that doesn't mean there wasn't one. I wouldn't have known because you never told me much about yourself. In the six weeks we were married, you didn't even want me to visit the office where you worked. Of course, I see now that it was a trick to keep me from knowing you too well so I couldn't find you when you ran away. I'm not the first to be fooled like that."

"I didn't trick you. I didn't fool you. How could I? I don't know you." Her head swung back and forth to deny everything he said. Deep inside she began to shake, but she managed to latch onto one thing he had said. "Six weeks?"

"That's how long we were married before you left, as I'm sure you recall."

"No, I've told you, I don't. Why won't you believe me?" She was interrupted by a knock on the door. He half-turned, opening a path for her. Gratefully, she stumbled past him to answer it, wrenching the door open and all but tumbling outside.

Mary was there, looking faintly irritated. "Are you busy talking shop with Mr Parker?" she asked. "Can't it wait? I thought you were going to come help... what's wrong with you?"

"No—nothing," Annie stammered, throwing a quick look over her shoulder. "I'm coming."

Flynn surged forward as if to stop her, but he paused, seeming to reconsider. "I'll see you later. We can talk then. I assume you'll be around."

If you're not, I'll find you. The threat was implicit in his voice and manner.

Gulping down a bubble of hysteria, Annie grabbed Mary's arm and rushed away. He didn't pursue her, and Annie was sure he had realized that on an island this size, there weren't many places to go. They would talk again soon, and he would expect her to have answers, but how could she answer questions about something of which she was ignorant?

"Are you all right?" Mary asked as Annie hustled her along to the staircase. "You're not getting the same flu that James has, are you? You've gone white as cake flour."

"Flu?" Annie gave her a wild look. She wished that was all that was wrong with her. At least flu could be easily cured. "No, I'm not sick. I'm fine."

Except that her mind was whirling with questions, her insides had gone sick with fear, and her legs could barely hold her up. How could she have been married to Flynn Parker? She didn't even know him. Did she? That was exactly the problem. She wasn't sure. He could be lying. But why would he?

She didn't realize how tightly she was clutching Mary's arm until the older woman flinched and covered Annie's cold fingers with her own. "Annie, honey, what is the matter with you? Did Mr Parker say something to upset you?"

Did he ever! Annie almost blurted out the truth but stopped herself in time. Mary was protective of Annie, more so since Annie's parents' deaths. Why upset her before Annie herself knew all the facts? "No, it's ... I'm all right."

"If you're sick, I can handle dinner by myself," Mary said worriedly, as they reached the bottom of the stairs and headed for the kitchen. By now, she was all but propping Annie up as they walked.

Annie wanted to say yes and hide in her room for the rest of the afternoon and evening. She wanted to think things through, then go ask Flynn Parker to explain—if he was in better control of his temper. She didn't want to see anyone just now, especially not him. But as much as she wanted to, she couldn't hide. She had duties and responsibilities in the hotel, and especially in the kitchen.

"I'm all right, Mary," she repeated, forcing herself to stand alone and drawing her composure around her like a cloak. She ran shaky hands over her face, then twisted her fingers together at her waist. "I guess I shouldn't have been running with Luis outside. Maybe it made me dizzy. I'll go splash some water on my face."

Before Mary could question that lame explanation, Annie fled to her small room in the back hallway and rushed into her bathroom. After washing her face and brushing her hair into a ponytail, she stood gripping the edge of the cool porcelain sink. She stared into her own wide, shocked eyes. It couldn't be true, could it?

Nausea rose again in her throat and she battled it down. She felt herself being pulled backward into the vortex of despair she had known two years ago. Her life had been shattered, and her struggles to rebuild it had taken all of her strength and determination. Only by focusing on each day, by concentrating on her work at the inn, had she managed to survive.

Now, if what Flynn Parker said was true, all her struggles had been for nothing. There was something in the past that she couldn't escape.

Annie closed her eyes and tried to clear her mind, to calm herself before going to the kitchen. Finally, she pushed herself away from the sink and left the room.

In the kitchen, she tied on an apron and turned to Mary, who was watching her in silent alarm. "Tell me what you want done."

Mary started to speak, then shook her head. Annie knew she was thinking that there was too much work to be done for her to press the issue, even though she was concerned. She gave Annie binsful of vegetables to be scrubbed and chopped and then returned to her own work.

Annie was grateful for the mindless task. She didn't have to think about what she was doing as her thoughts replayed the scene with Flynn and tried to view it calmly. It was obvious that he knew her. He had called her by her full name. He knew she had been in Seattle two years ago for a period of time that had lasted almost two months.

His claim that they were married was completely ridiculous, though. It had to be.

Carlos and Luis walked through on their way home to the little cottage they occupied out back. There were two others, one in which Mary and James lived and one for Velma, the waitress.

Velma came in and began filling water pitchers and salt and pepper shakers for the tables.

Despite the inn's desperate need for paying guests, Annie was grateful that there were only fifteen currently in the hotel. The evening's chores would be light. As much as she wanted to hide in the kitchen, Annie knew she couldn't. When she was finished helping Mary, she went to her room to change clothes. As she sifted through the clothes in her closet, her hand fell on her favorite outfit, a white skirt and wide-necked silk sweater. Wearing it always seemed to give her confidence, although strangely, she didn't remember buying it. She had found it in her suitcase when she had returned from

Seattle. It was beautiful, but too fancy for one of the inn's informal, family-style dinners.

She bypassed the outfit and settled on a gauzy broomstick skirt and satin-trimmed T-shirt of moss green. She braided her hair neatly out of her face and went to act as hostess in the dining room.

Flynn Parker didn't show up for dinner until most of the other guests had arrived and been seated. When she spotted him, Annie was standing by the windowed kitchen door. At last, she had the opportunity to observe him. Their first encounter had been such a shock that she had come away with only sensations—heat, anger, power—but no clear picture of what he looked like or what kind of man he was.

He was tall, with wide shoulders and long limbs. His hands were big, like a basketball player's, his movements smooth and coordinated. His thick, dark hair was cut short and combed straight back from his forehead. It served to emphasize the sharp edges of his high cheekbones and the intensity of his eyes as they swept the room.

Even dressed casually in dark trousers, white shirt and a gray suede sports jacket, he looked like a man of strength and determination. Annie felt prickles of alarm at the thought of facing him again even as she found herself unwillingly fascinated by him. It was interesting to watch the reactions of the other diners, mostly retired couples. The women sat up and smiled, fluffing their hair. The men sat up and sucked in their stomachs.

Flynn didn't seem to notice anyone. He chose to sit alone at a table overlooking the terrace. He glanced out at the gathering dusk, then turned and searched the room until he spied her hovering by the door. As if pulled by the force of his will, Annie walked over and handed him a menu. Their dinner selections were very basic. Mary preferred to rely on standards, which she cooked to perfection.

Flynn glanced at it, made his selection, then asked, "When can we talk?" He tapped his fingertips on the white linen tablecloth as he waited for her answer.

This time she was ready for him. He wasn't going to take her by surprise. She knew what to expect and she knew how to answer. She folded the menu and placed it in the crook of her elbow as she met his direct gaze. "Right after the dinner crowd clears out. We can go into my office."

"Fine."

Back straight, Annie turned away and began assisting Velma, but she was aware of him all through dinner. He ate slowly and methodically, but whenever she passed his table, she sensed the impatience in him.

At last, the guests drifted off to their evening's entertainment, television in the lounge, dancing in the common room with music provided by a stereo system. Annie knew Beatrice and Velma could take care of anything that came up, so she saw the last of the guests on their way out of the dining room, then turned to tell Flynn that she was ready. There was no need. He had moved from his table and stood inches from her.

"Oh, you startled me."

"Well, it's not the first time today, is it?" he said grimly. "Shall we go?"

Quickly regaining her composure, she led him into the hotel's foyer and behind the front desk. It was being manned by Martin, freshly cleaned up for the honor and fitted out in a fresh shirt and one of James's old ties. She opened the door into an office that had once been a large closet. She moved to sit behind her desk and gestured to a comfortable chair that had been shoved into a tiny space beside a file cabinet. "Please sit down."

Flynn closed the door, took one look at the small room and the chair and said, "I'll stand."

Although she wished they were on the same level, Annie was convinced she could retain control of the situation. She perched on the edge of her own chair and clasped her fingers together on the desk blotter. "Let's try to talk about this calmly and rationally," she said and was quite proud of her cool tone.

Flynn stared at her for several seconds before he spoke. "You gave me the damnedest shock of my life today."

Annie waited for him to go on, but then realized that he wasn't going to apologize for frightening her. Perhaps he thought she deserved the shock. That thought strengthened her determination to see this through.

"I'm not lying to you," she said in a level tone. "I don't remember you, marrying you..." She almost added, "loving you," but stopped herself in time.

He walked over and perched on the edge of her desk. It made her feel small and vulnerable. To overcome the feeling, she leaned back in the chair and lifted her chin.

"You *were* in Seattle," he stated.

"Yes. Yes, I was."

"In February and March, two years ago."

She licked her lips. "I was doing an internship with Heritage Inns, but I...I don't recall anything about that, either."

"I find that hard to believe." He ran his hand over his face. "This whole damn thing is hard to believe."

"It's true. I keep telling you it's true." Why wouldn't he believe her? She found it just as fantastic to believe that she had been married to a man, slept with him, made love with him, for goodness' sake—and yet had no memory of him. If she let herself dwell on that too closely, it would drive her out of her mind.

He gave her his steady, commanding stare. "Why don't you start at the beginning?"

She wasn't quite sure where that was, but after a rebellious moment of silence, she plunged in. "My parents and my uncle owned this inn. Now he and I own it. I grew up here and the understanding was that I would run it someday. My dad thought I needed experience with a national chain, though, so I went into the internship program that Heritage has established. The first part was spent in Los Angeles, then I was to transfer to the new Heritage Place Hotel in Seattle. I came home on my days off."

Her words began coming more slowly. Her deep blue eyes were full of distress as she stopped to swallow a lump in her throat. "On one of those..." She stopped to take a breath and steady herself. "On one of those days off, just before I was supposed to go to Seattle to continue my internship, I came home for a few days." She fell silent, recalling her distress at being away from the island, at being assigned to the internship in a strange city. "My parents were flying into Santa Barbara for supplies. My dad was a pilot, flew his own plane." Her lips tightened as she once again faced the painful memories. At least she could talk about it now. She was making progress. "I stood on the landing strip and saw them off. At takeoff, something went wrong with the plane. It went down on the rocks at the east end of the island."

Flynn jerked visibly and his hand opened, reaching toward her. "They were killed," he said, his voice dulled by horror.

"Yes." Annie pressed her fingers to her mouth, pushing back the sobs that threatened to erupt. Finally, she gulped them down, but they burned like fire in her throat.

"And you saw it."

"Yes. We...we buried them under the pines. I closed the inn and a...a friend took me to Seattle by boat. I don't know what I was thinking then," she continued slowly. "I must have had some idea in mind that I needed to finish my commitment to the internship program." She glanced up and met his searching gaze. "At least that's what I've come to believe. I don't remember anything after my parents' funeral. The next thing I recall is walking down a street in Seattle with my suitcases in my hands. It was exactly two months later.''

Flynn began pacing the tiny office. ''That must have been the day you left my apartment. I returned from a business trip and found you gone. You'd left behind everything I'd given you, including your wedding ring.''

''So you divorced me? For abandonment?''

His look was swift and sharp. ''No.''

''You mean we're still married?''

''Yes.''

''Why?'' Somehow the knowledge that she might still be married, *was* still married, to this stranger hadn't occurred to her. It was the most unnerving of all the shocks she had received on this strange day.

''Maybe I wanted to find out why you'd done it. Why you'd left me without a word.''

Annie didn't think that was the whole reason. ''If I'd known about you, I'd have written you a note,'' she said grimly. ''I came back here and the only thing I have of Seattle is a picture someone took of me at the Space Needle.''

''I took that picture.'' Flynn reached for his wallet and pulled out a photograph. ''I asked a passerby to take one of us together.'' He flipped it onto the desk before her and Annie stared into her own image. The mouth was smiling, but the eyes were incredibly sad. Her first reaction was sorrow and her second one was to wonder what a man like Flynn Parker had seen in a woman who looked like that.

She examined his face in the photograph. His expression seemed to be cautious, and yet possessive, too, as was the arm he had placed around her shoulders. She wondered if the gesture had been for the benefit of the camera, or if he'd actually been that protective of her. She looked up and met his fierce, demanding eyes. She wasn't sure she wanted to know.

Annie pushed the photograph away. Flynn picked it up and returned it to his wallet, then stood watching her with a brooding expression. "How could you have forgotten everything from that time?" His tone was suspicious, accusing, doubtful.

Anger spurted through Annie and she rose to face him as she splayed a hand across her chest. "Do you think I wasn't terrified? I came back to conscious life in a city I didn't know. I had to ask a street vendor what city I was in. The man looked at me as if I was insane."

The expression on Flynn's dark face told her he still didn't believe her. "You must have gone straight to Heritage Inn headquarters and quit your job."

"It was the only thing I could think of to do. Once I found out I was in Seattle, I knew why I was there, but when I learned the date and realized I had lost two months of my life, I was terrified."

That was an understatement. She had been one breath away from screaming hysteria.

Annie clutched her arms across her waist and turned away from him. At the Heritage office, her co-workers had made comments about her not having to work now that she had a wealthy husband, but since she had no memory of them, either, she had ignored them and fled. "I called a friend and he flew up to get me, then rented a car and drove me home. I waited at another hotel for him." It had been James, home on a few days' leave. He had been shocked to receive her call because neither he nor Mary had heard from her during her time in Seattle. He had rushed to help her because Annie had been incoherent with panic.

Flynn's eyes were narrowed as he stared at her. She thought he was going to ask who the friend was, but instead he looked around impatiently and said, "Let's get out of here. I'm getting claustrophobia in this place."

She blinked at him. "Out?"

"Outside. I saw a path down to the beach. We'll go there." He jerked the door open and waited for her to join him. "Come on."

"It's dark," she protested, but he was already into the lobby. She jumped up and hurried along behind him. Darn it, why was he doing this?

"Got a jacket close by?"

"I'll get one," she sighed. It was more than obvious that there was no point in arguing. She hurried to her room, grabbed a denim jacket and met him at the front door. When the first blast of cool, bracing air hit her, Annie decided it might have been a good idea after all. The small office had been too full of doubts and unspoken accusations. Out on the beach the emotions between them might not seem so insurmountable.

Couples strolled on the lawn and several of them waved as Flynn and Annie made their way down the steps, across the lawn and onto the gently sloping path that wound down to the beach. Once they reached the small cove, Flynn turned west, into the setting sun. He shortened his strides to match hers and Annie was amazed that he possessed that much patience and consideration.

They walked in silence for a few minutes and Annie was grateful for the respite. She looked out at the inky blackness of the ocean and then up to the diamond-studded velvet sky. All her life, she had been able to consider the vastness of it and feel her problems shrinking to a manageable size. That wasn't going to happen tonight.

Her muscles tensed when Flynn spoke again. "How long did it take you to recover your memory?"

She clenched her fists in frustration. "Haven't you heard a word I've said? I *never* recovered it. I was wild on the way home trying to recall anything, anything at all from those lost weeks, but it was a blank. It's still a blank. I went straight to my doctor in Santa Barbara. He said I have an amnesiac condition called fugue."

Flynn stopped and turned to face her. Even in the near-darkness, she caught the gleam of disbelief in his eyes. "Fugue? That's a musical term."

"It's also a psychiatric term." She should know. She had done a great deal of study on it in the past two years. "It's a flight from reality in which a person will assume a personality, a whole life different from their normal one. Actions will seem rational, but are forgotten when the mind is ready to face reality once again. It's usually brought on by a severe psychological shock.''

"Your parents' deaths.''

Did she hear a softening in his tone? When she glanced at his controlled expression, she knew she'd imagined it.

"And being in the internship program. It was difficult for me. There was a great deal of information and training that I simply don't need to run an inn this size. It was as if my brain was in overload. Also, I hated being away from this island.''

He frowned. "But your parents died here.''

"There are more happy memories here than sad ones.''

"So you're saying you remember everything before their deaths?''

"And except for that two-month period, everything since.''

Flynn tucked his chin against his chest and looked down at the rocky beach for a minute. When he glanced up, his eyes were hard. "In other words, I'm the only thing you've forgotten.''

A hundred emotions buffeted her—among them compassion, defensiveness, stubbornness. Her strongest one was reluctance to explain herself to a man she didn't know despite their apparent history. She lifted her hands helplessly. "So it seems.''

"Will you ever remember?''

She shrugged, then realized he couldn't see her in the gathering dusk and said, "I don't know. The doctors I've consulted say I may never recall any of that time because in my mind, that wasn't really me living that life."

Flynn made a growling sound low in his throat. "This whole thing is just too damned hard to believe. Apparently, I was married to a counterfeit."

Unaccountably, that hurt. Annie snapped at him. "It's just as hard for me to believe that I'm married to you."

"Do you want proof?"

"Yes. Yes, I do. Something that can't be doubted."

"Fine. I'll have my secretary send our marriage certificate."

"Fine." Annie turned away from him and stared out at the swelling surf. Silence stretched between them. Annie knew she should go back to the hotel and take care of evening chores, see if any of the guests needed anything before retiring. It was getting dark and the path up from the beach could be treacherous at night, but she lingered. She had read much about fugue and its manifestations, but she still had many questions.

"What was I like?" she asked. "When we were . . ."

"Married," Flynn supplied for her in a furious tone. "When we lived together as husband and wife? When we traded off time in the bathroom to shower or showered together? When we had breakfast together and stood hip to hip at the bathroom sink brushing our teeth? When you dropped off the dry cleaning and I picked it up? You mean when we were *married*?"

Shocked at his vehement tone and the startling mental pictures his words created, Annie nodded. "Yes, all right. When we were married, what was I like? What brought us together?"

"Does this mean you're admitting I'm telling the truth?"

"I'm not admitting anything—yet, but I can't think of any reason you would lie—but then, I don't really know you, do I?"

"No. You don't know me at all, and even though you want to know what you were like then, I'm not going to answer that question tonight," he said, taking her arm as he turned toward the inn. "You've been through enough for one day, and so, by damn, have I!"

CHAPTER THREE

"THIS is the craziest thing I've ever heard." James Fredericks stared at Annie as if she had suddenly grown two heads.

"You're telling me! I'm still in shock." Annie made an effort to control the note of hysteria that crept into her voice. She gulped and ran her damp palms down the legs of the hunter green trousers that matched her sweater, then checked to see if she had left streaks on the fabric.

She had to calm down, she told herself, settling back into the patio chair that faced the lounge where James was reclining. He was still recovering from the flu but he had insisted that he had to get out of the house. He had tolerated Mary's fussing as she had settled him on their tiny front patio, tucked a knitted afghan around his legs and made him a cup of tea before hurrying off to work.

Annie had come over to talk to him as soon as she saw that Mary was gone. She wasn't exactly hiding from Mary, but she had wanted to discuss things with James first. For all her practical level-headedness, Mary would fuss and hover over Annie once she learned about Flynn, whereas James would listen and try to help her find a solution.

Annie gave him a worried look, hoping she wasn't burdening him. He seemed to be feeling a little better, but his face still had a grayish cast to it. He shouldn't spend too long out of bed.

She shook her head in dismay and tucked in strands of hair that had escaped from her French braid. "I shouldn't be bothering you with this when you're not well yet."

"Don't be stupid," he said gruffly. "Who else would you tell but your best friend?"

She smiled shakily and nodded, then ran a hand over her exhausted face as she sighed. "You're right. It's been such a shock that I can't seem to get my thoughts straight." She hadn't slept all night, but had tossed in her bed watching the red digital numbers on her alarm clock switch from one to another, silently clicking away the hours.

"Do you think he's telling the truth?"

"I..."

"Come on, gut feeling. Is he telling the truth?"

"It seems so, but he says he's going to have his secretary send a copy of our marriage certificate so I'll be sure."

"Then what?"

She threw her hands wide, almost upsetting the untouched cup of tea. She fumbled it into its saucer. "Then I don't know! I just don't know."

"You could divorce him. This is California, remember? Divorces are as easy to get as fishing licenses."

"Yes, I could," she said slowly. She had considered that during her long night of tossing and turning. She had always wanted a marriage like the one her parents had. They shared everything, never losing the art of communicating with each other.

They had been very much in love. The day they died, they had walked to the plane holding hands.

Her parents had taught her to finish what she started. Somehow, divorcing Flynn would seem as though she was abandoning him all over again, running away from her responsibilities. And yet, if she had no memory of him, if the woman he had married had been Annie Locke in name only, was the marriage valid?

True, the first time she had left him, she hadn't remembered anything about him, still didn't, for that matter. In a way, she understood the fascination he had held for her in the past two years. Her subconscious mind must have remembered something that her conscious mind still couldn't recall and had sought information about him in the hotel trade magazines and newsletters.

Now, meeting him, seeing what kind of man Flynn Parker was, she knew that he wouldn't let her go easily—at least not until he had the answers he sought. But why would he want to stay married to her?

"I wonder why he's stayed married to you," James went on.

"That's another thing I don't know." She shook her head in a sharp negative, not surprised that he could read her thoughts. He'd been doing it since she was born. Three years older than she, he had been a big brother to her in every way but blood.

"You've got some time to decide what to do. He must not be in a hurry, or he would have found you sooner."

Annie sat up and looked at him, her eyes wide. Of course. Why *hadn't* Flynn tried to find her? It wouldn't have been that hard for someone with money and resources at his command. "I hadn't thought of that."

James rolled his eyes in comical sympathy. "Hm, I don't wonder why. All you did yesterday was find out you've got a husband you don't remember marrying. That should be enough to make everything else fly out of your head, and besides . . . is that him?"

"What?" She turned quickly to look where James indicated. Flynn was coming around the corner of the inn, his stride long and purposeful. He didn't stop when he saw them, but headed straight in their direction.

James tossed the afghan off his legs and swung his feet to the ground.

Annie threw out her hand to stop him. "Don't get up. You're not well."

"You think I'm going to meet this guy while I'm lying around like an invalid? Think again."

Annie, too, scrambled to her feet and stood close beside him. She knew what James meant. Flynn wasn't the type of man before whom one would like to show weakness, and she felt that was all she'd shown him so far.

She had only known him a day—at least, this time—but she was learning to read his body language. The straight set of his shoulders, the lift of his chin said he was coming to find her and she'd better be ready for him. Her heart began to pummel against her ribs. Jolted, she realized that it was from excited anticipation rather than dread.

When Flynn approached them, his gaze was fixed on her. He ignored James. "I've been looking for you."

She attempted to swallow the lump that had formed in her throat. "Have . . . have you?"

"Why don't you show me around your island?"

It didn't seem to occur to him that she might have work to do. In automatic self-defense, she was about to tell him that she was busy when she caught sight of the lines of strain around his eyes. They were twins of her own. His night must have been as sleepless as hers. He was dressed in black jeans and a heavy sweater of dark blue that made his eyes seem even more impenetrable than they had the day before.

"Around the island?"

"You don't look too busy." At last his gaze settled on James, who straightened to the military correctness he'd learned from six years in the Marines.

Struggling to sort her thoughts and feelings, Annie indicated her friend. "This is James Fredericks. James, Flynn Parker."

The two men sized each other up. James pulled his arm from around her and held out his hand. Flynn hesitated for an instant before shaking it. The hard expression in Flynn's green eyes seemed to soften as if James had done something to gain his respect. Confused, Annie looked from one to the other of them. Some kind of silent, male communication was going on between them.

She was disconcerted to see a spark of humor appear in James's eyes. "Go ahead, Annie," he said. "I'm going back to bed. I've been up too long. You don't need to stay with me."

She blinked and glanced at Flynn in time to see satisfaction come and go in his expression.

"Shall we go, then, Annie?"

"I have work to do."

"There aren't so many guests at your inn right now that your presence is required every minute," Flynn said with the calm firmness that she was discovering was his usual way of dealing with things.

"No, but there are morning chores to be done."

"Go with him, Annie," James urged. "It seems you two need to talk."

Annie gave her friend an irritated glare, but she couldn't think of anything to say to him except to mutter, "Traitor," under her breath as Flynn took her arm and led her away.

"You told him about us?" Flynn asked when they had walked out of James's hearing.

"Of course. He's my best friend." To her dismay, she discovered that she was very much aware of the warmth of his hand through the sleeves of her sweater and tan corduroy jacket. It seemed as though her body was taking over for her brain now that she was recovering from yesterday's shock. She eased her arm from his grasp and strode along beside him.

"I've never known a man and woman be best friends without it leading to something more."

"Then this is a first for you, isn't it?" she asked sweetly.

He ignored her sardonic question. "Are you in love with him?"

Annie rounded on him, stopping him in his tracks. She tilted her head back so she could look him straight in the eye. "You seem to think I have difficulty with truthfulness as well as memory. Everything I've told you is true, and so is this." She pointed a finger at his chest. "James is like a brother to me. No more, and certainly no less."

Flynn studied the defiance in her eyes, the angle of her chin and the color she could feel climbing her cheeks. "I see," he said and then he changed the subject as if, once he had the information he needed, he could forget about it. "Why don't you show me the recreational facilities?"

Annie took a breath to steady her temper, something she had the feeling she would be doing often while she was around Flynn. The past twenty-four hours had been an unbelievable roller coaster of emotions, and it wasn't over yet.

"Let's go to the tennis courts. Some of the guests are having doubles games this afternoon and Carlos tells me there's a hole in the net."

"And you'll mend it? Where's your maintenance man?"

"Carlos *is* the maintenance man, but he has other things to do this morning."

"Then I'll help you."

Annie didn't even bother to argue. It would have done no good whatsoever.

At the tennis courts, she found a ball of cord in a storage locker and knelt to tie off the ragged ends of the tear and weave in a replacement. There were several such mended places in the open fabric.

As she worked, Flynn looked down the length of the net and said, "You need a new net."

Her fingers tightened on the cord. "This one will last a while longer."

"Not much."

Her blue eyes darkened dangerously as she looked at him. "When I can afford one, I'll buy it." She grasped two ends of broken cord and tried to pull them snugly together.

Flynn rested on his heels, took the pieces in his own fingers and held them steady. Annie paused, aware of the way his skin had brushed hers, of the square tips of his long fingers holding the net so she could mend it. It was a small thing and she couldn't have said why it disturbed her. Without meeting his eyes, she hurriedly finished the knot.

"If you're short on money, maybe you need an investor."

That rocked her back on her heels. It was bad enough having to deal with her absentee uncle who was in frequent need of ready cash. There was no way she wanted to answer to anyone else. "No," she said quickly. "It's been a hard winter, that's all. We're financially stable as long as I don't spend money on unnecessary expenses."

"Annie, quality is everything in the hotel business." His lips twitched. "Or at least the appearance of quality. People don't pay these kinds of prices to play tennis on a court with a mended net."

He was right, of course, but she didn't want to admit it. "The court itself is smooth and in good repair. That's all that's needed."

She grabbed the ball of cord and tried to break it away from the knot. Flynn pulled a small knife from his pocket, flipped out a blade and cut the cord.

A small indentation appeared between Annie's brows as she looked at the knife. She had seen it yesterday in his room. Flynn pushed the blade in and held the small weapon out to her. The pearl handle shone with a dull gloss in the morning light. "Do you recognize this?"

"No." Her voice was low and troubled. "Should I?"

"You bought it for me." He slipped it into his pocket, then stood up. He reached down, took the ball of cord from her suddenly lifeless fingers and strolled over to stow it in the locker.

There it was again. That wall between them. He remembered everything and she remembered nothing. Desperate with frustration, she rose and steadied herself against the pole holding the net. "Why would I have bought you a pocketknife?"

"You said I needed one."

Her father had always carried one, finding a dozen uses for it as he worked around the inn. The thought that she had given him the type of gift she equated with her father disturbed her. It suggested that in some part of her mind she had considered her marriage to Flynn to be permanent. Is that what *he* thought?

Annie looked out at the horizon for a second before she asked, "Did you look for me?"

If her question surprised him, he didn't show it. He was silent until she brought her gaze to his. The breeze ruffled his hair, tossing it across his forehead. Absently, he smoothed it back. "It was three days before I knew you were gone."

"When you returned from your business trip?"

"Yes. I was in Hawaii. I wanted you to go with me, but you wouldn't fly and I certainly couldn't go by sea. It would have taken too long."

"And when you returned, I was gone."

"Along with all your clothes. The only things you left were the things I'd bought you, or that you'd bought after we were married."

Her subconscious mind had been making a very definite break between one part of her life and another. She had read of that happening. Annie shivered. It wasn't easy being a textbook case of such a strange malady.

"By the time I realized you were really gone, had left the city, almost a week had passed. The people at the Heritage Place Hotel knew nothing of your background, and the only address they had was a post office box in Santa Barbara. When I checked that out, the box had been rented to someone else. And then..."

The grim note that had crept into his voice drew her around to look at him. "Then?" she prompted.

"My father died. Heart attack. No one even suspected there was anything wrong, though he'd pushed himself too hard for years. I had funeral arrangements to make, my mother and sister to care for, and then, of course, there was the corporation. There were hundreds of employees . . . we were in the middle of a big expansion that had been very important to my father, and right after that, corporate sharks moved in for a takeover bid.''

Although he stated his list of responsibilities in a matter-of-fact way, there was no disguising the bleakness in his tone when he spoke of his father.

''I heard about your father's death . . . when I once again began taking an interest in what was going on in the hotel business. It must have been a terrible shock. I'm sorry.''

Flynn acknowledged her expression of sympathy with a nod and a tightening of his jaw. Annie felt that the hurt of his father's death must have gone very deep. They must have been close. His relationship with his father was the type of thing Flynn would have discussed with her, his wife. How long would it be before he felt at ease enough with her again to discuss it?

With a start, Annie drew herself up short. She was venturing into areas she didn't want to think about. She tucked her hands beneath the sides of her jacket and focused on what he had said. Everything in his life had changed in a matter of days. He had obviously dealt with that type of loss far more easily than she had. It made her feel like a weakling, but it also flooded her with a strange mixture of sympathy and admiration for him.

''I could have hired a detective,'' he continued. ''And I intended to as soon as things settled down, but things never settled down, and . . .''

"You were furious with me," Annie stated with a flash of insight. "And your pride was hurt."

Flynn looked away from her, the strong bones in his jaw working once again as if he was biting back words. "Yeah. Never thought of myself as a proud man, but I am. I didn't like getting kicked in the teeth."

"So you left things as they were?" That didn't fit with what she was learning of his personality. He was decisive and sure of what he wanted, yet he had allowed his marriage to remain in a state of uncertainty for two years. Annie gave him a troubled frown. He wasn't telling her everything.

"I left things as they were until now. As I said, there was no time to deal with it until I could take a break from work. I had decided that as soon as I returned home I would do whatever was necessary to find you and resolve the marriage one way or another."

Annie rubbed the back of her wrist across her forehead. "I feel like I'm hearing about the actions of a stranger. I . . . I am, in a way. The woman who left you like that wasn't me."

Flynn squinted into the bright sunlight. "I'm beginning to realize that."

A wave of relief washed over Annie. "So now that you've found me, even though it was accidental, the marriage is resolved, or maybe I should say dissolved. There's no reason for us to stay married."

"There might be."

"What possible reason could there be? All we have to do is file for a quiet divorce . . ."

"Why rush into a divorce?"

Annie threw her hands in the air. "We obviously rushed into marriage, why can't we get out of it just as easily?"

One of Flynn's dark brows lifted as he answered, "You just said yourself that the woman I married isn't who you really are."

"That's right," Annie answered slowly. She felt that she was maneuvering her way across a mine field.

"Then why would I want to dump you before I get to know you?"

"Because you don't know..." Annie's words ground to a halt. She held a hand to her forehead. This circular reasoning was beginning to make her dizzy. She pursed her lips. "Are you purposefully trying to confuse me?"

His wide shoulders lifted in a shrug. "No. You're already confused. I'm trying to help you clarify your thinking."

"Much more of this and smoke will start coming out my ears." She turned and started walking toward the inn. "I've got work to do."

"You were supposed to show me around."

She kept on walking. "Later."

"You're running away."

Flynn's hard statement fell at her heels like bricks. She spun around to face him. He hadn't moved, still stood several feet away, but she felt as if he was looming over her. "I would like to see this resolved as soon as possible."

"By resolved, you mean we'll do things your way." His tone told her he didn't find that plan appealing.

She lifted her chin as she felt heat begin to rise in her face. "I don't see why not."

He didn't answer her, but his eyes darkened and she saw a nameless emotion shifting in his expression. "I wondered if you had a temper. You never had one... before. You were quiet. Controlled."

"I keep telling you that wasn't the real me. This is the real me. Surely you don't want to stay married to a shrew."

"*I* didn't call you a shrew. I only said you have a temper. Surely that's not something a husband shouldn't say."

"How would I know what a husband should or shouldn't say?" she asked, fully exasperated.

"My experience is limited, too," he answered smoothly. "We'd better find out together just what husbands *and* wives are supposed to do before there's any talk of divorce."

Annie pressed her hands to her temples. This was driving her mad. He set verbal traps for her no matter which way she turned, and she invariably fell into them. Perhaps she hadn't left him the first time because of emotional storms on her part, but because his sheer determination and force of will had driven her off!

"Maybe we should just let that remain a mystery," she suggested.

"Maybe you'd better keep your promise and show me around your island."

"Oh, all right," she said in an ungracious tone. "You've seen the tennis court. Let's walk over to the golf course. We've got sets of clubs and we can probably find you a partner." She started to swing away from him, heading toward the green area that Martin and Carlos tended so carefully, but Flynn caught her arm. With a startled breath, she tried to pull away, but his fingers tightened on her wrist and drew her toward him.

"Don't you play anymore?"

Puzzled, she shook her head. "What? Golf?"

"That's right."

"I've never played in my life," she answered. Again, she tried to tug away from him, but it was like trying to resist the law of gravity. He ignored her struggles and pulled her close until they stood toe-to-toe. His look was sharp, intense as a surgeon's blade. She felt his warmth and power through the thickness of her sweater and jacket.

"I taught you myself. You were good at it."

She shook her head, once, then again. "No. I've never been very good at sports."

"You were playing soccer yesterday."

He *had* seen her. Her tongue touched the corner of her mouth, and interest kindled in Flynn's eyes. His hands eased so that he was barely touching her, holding her only with his will. Annie didn't know when the atmosphere had become charged with such tension, but it had come, hard and fast, like the heat lightning that sometimes hit the coast. It wasn't angry tension, though. It was desire. She wanted to break it. She was *going* to break it, but her gaze settled on his lips and she wondered what they would feel like against her own. Would her body remember what her mind had forgotten? Sensual heat ran in waves below the surface of her skin.

"Annie?" His voice seemed to be coming from a distance, low and awesome, like thunder. "You were playing soccer yesterday."

"Oh...oh, yes. I was playing with Luis. He was lonely, wishing for a playmate."

"I see."

The deep timbre of Flynn's voice sent shivers through her. How could he convey such powerful desire in only two words? How had he been able to command the forces of nature, changing the brightness of morning into something as heated and dark as words whispered between midnight lovers?

Somehow, his arm was around her waist, drawing her to him. His left hand held her right one. His fingertips slipped along the inside of her wrist, sliding the sleeves of her garments out of his way, exposing the pale flesh. He rubbed her skin, sensitizing it with a slight roughness.

Hazily, Annie wondered how a man who worked at a desk could have calluses, but the drifting thought didn't establish itself in her mind. She was aware of him, of his closeness, the heat of his touch, his scent, which made her think of sea spray—fresh and clean.

His fingers found her pulse, which skittered and bounced like the ball on a spinning roulette wheel.

"You were fulfilling the wish of a little boy. That's good of you. How about the wishes of men?"

She watched his lips form the words. Was he going to kiss her? "I don't know what you mean," she breathed. *When* was he going to kiss her?

"Would you fulfill my wish, Annie?"

"What is it?" She was having trouble keeping her eyes open. She wanted to let them drift shut as she concentrated on feeling the sensations Flynn was calling forth. Everything else in the world seemed to be blocked out as she focused on his voice and touch.

"I want you to kiss me. That's not too much for a husband to ask, is it? One kiss in two years? I haven't been such a demanding husband, have I, that you would refuse me a kiss?"

Annie finally surrendered, letting her eyes close. She lifted her chin so that her mouth was only a breath away from his. "Certainly not." The words were almost a whimper, so badly did she want his lips on hers.

Silently, he rewarded her, bringing his mouth to hers, only to turn it aside at the last second and settle it on her wrist. Her pulse went mad beneath his lips, but she couldn't help the tiny moan of distress that escaped her lips. Wasn't he going to kiss her?

With his lips against her skin, he looked up and met her eyes. Heat was there, and triumph. Before she could form a conclusion about the significance of that, Flynn had placed her hand on his shoulder, tilted her mouth to his and taken possession of it.

Annie sighed with pleasure as she moved her arm up and around his neck, driving her fingers into his rich, dark hair. One part of her mind tried to recall if she had ever felt this before, ever kissed him like this before, while another part of her mind decided it didn't matter and revelled in the moment.

He tasted wonderful, like every delicious thing she had ever known. He was wildest excitement and deepest security. With only the touch of his mouth on her own, he sent spiraling swirls of light and color through her mind.

Annie knew what her body had been trying to tell her. This man had been her lover. She didn't remember, but she *knew*.

He drew away and Annie chased his lips with her own. He rewarded her responsiveness with small, biting kisses that made her lips tingle. "Annie," he said. "You have to tell me something."

Her eyes were closed. She was wrapped around him as tightly as a flag around a flagpole on a windless day. Her hands were in his hair and her lips against his. Unconsciously, she lifted her chin so he could reach the vulnerable underside of her jaw. He placed kisses there that melted her all the way to her bones. She did the same to him, earning a small grunt of satisfaction.

"What do you need to know, Flynn?"

"Have there been other men since me? Other men since you left me?"

Annie felt as if she had been drenched with ice water. With a gasp, she stepped out of his arms. She touched her mouth, which still throbbed from his kisses. "What do you mean?"

His eyes narrowed, hardening his face, but Annie was gratified to see that his lips were as full and no doubt throbbed as much as her own. She threw back her head and met his eyes defiantly.

"You never kissed me like that before," he said in a voice as rough as sandpaper. "Like you wanted to crawl right inside my skin. You were a gentle lover, tentative. Has someone taught you how wild things can get between a man and a woman?"

Fury such as she had never known spurted through her, blurring Annie's vision. "No!" she shouted at him. "No! There have been no other men, not that it would be any of your business."

He was unruffled by her outburst. "Everything about you is my business, Annie. You're my wife."

"I still need proof of that." She whirled away from him.

Her hands flew to her cheeks, which burned with embarrassment. What had possessed her to kiss him like that? He was right about her response. She would have been tearing his clothes off any second if he hadn't stopped her. Although she had lashed out at him, most of her anger was directed at herself.

She was turning to him, ready to finish their argument, when she heard her name being called. Luis was flying across the lawn, his small legs pumping furiously.

Annie rushed to him, Flynn at her heels. Luis was running so hard, he barreled into her. She righted him and it took a few seconds for him to catch his breath before he blurted, "Mary's sick. She needs you in the kitchen. My mama said come quick."

Annie didn't bother to ask questions, but grabbed his hand and dashed away. Flynn kept pace with her and she gave him a furious look. "This is hotel business, Flynn. You needn't concern yourself with it."

"I'm in the hotel business, remember?"

"Not this one."

He didn't react to her anger. "Maybe I can help," he said calmly.

When they reached the kitchen door, she swung through first, ignoring him. Mary was seated at the worktable, her head resting on her hands, Beatrice hovering over her. Mary lifted a white face as Annie and Flynn rushed in.

"She's got the same flu that James has," Beatrice said, her dark eyes full of worry. She wiped Mary's face with a damp cloth. "But she's insisting that she must finish preparing lunch."

Annie rushed to her friend. "You've got to get to bed right away and stay there until you feel better."

"Who's going to cook?" Mary asked. "Not you. Beatrice can help, but she's only accustomed to cooking for three."

"Don't worry about that," Annie insisted. "We'll think of something." She couldn't imagine what, but her main concern was Mary. In her whole life, she had never seen Mary with more than a slight cold.

"What do you do when she takes time off?" Flynn asked. "You must have a backup chef."

"Yes," Annie said, casting him a distracted glance. She was still angry with him and embarrassed over her reaction to his kiss, but she would think about that later. "Lately, James has been taking over, but he can't this time."

Flynn nodded and walked over to Mary. He bent easily and picked her up as if she weighed no more than a feather pillow. "Let's get you home," he said. "Then *I'll* take over the kitchen."

CHAPTER FOUR

"This really isn't your responsibility, Flynn, it's mine, and—"

"But you can't cook—unless that was part of your fugue amnesia, too." He gave her one of the disbelieving looks that Annie was coming to hate.

They were standing in the middle of the kitchen, facing each other over mounds of vegetables to be washed and prepared.

Flynn had carried Mary to her cottage, where James had greeted her with alarmed distress. He was feeling well enough to look after her, so Flynn and Annie had left the two of them alone.

Once in the kitchen, she had discovered that Flynn really meant it when he said he would take over. In spite of her protests, he had already been upstairs to exchange his sweater for a blue striped oxford-cloth shirt whose sleeves he rolled up above his elbows. Now he was flipping through Mary's recipes, which she kept in a three-ring binder.

Annie knew she should be grateful for any help at this point with lunch only an hour away and dinner looming on the horizon, but since Flynn had walked into her life, she had been scrambling for her footing, and felt that she was losing it rapidly.

He laid the binder open on the counter and regarded Annie with interest. "Well, was it part of your amnesia?"

Annie drew her lips together and lifted her chin defiantly, not liking the emphasis he put on the last word. He still didn't believe her.

"No. I can't cook," she admitted, although by now she wouldn't have been surprised to discover that when she had lived with Flynn she had been a world-class chef capable of turning out exquisite gourmet meals. "But I suppose you can." Her tone barely rescued itself from sounding sulky.

Flynn straightened and placed his hands on his hips. "My dad insisted that I learn every part of the business from the front desk to the kitchen. I spent six months at a cooking school in Paris. I'm not a chef, but I can handle things—with your help."

"Since it's my kitchen in my inn, I expect to help," she said tightly.

As if she hadn't spoken, Flynn went on, "Obviously, we'll have to start with lunch." He glanced around and spied the stockpot simmering on the stove. "Looks like Mary was making vegetable soup. We'll have that with sandwiches. I'll start dessert." He flipped the pages of the binder until he found the one he wanted, then glanced at Annie. "If you tell the guests about Mary's illness, they'll probably be understanding and not demand too much in the way of extra perks at lunch."

While Flynn was giving these instructions, Annie was reminding herself to be calm. After all, he was accustomed to giving orders and having people leap to obey. He simply couldn't help taking over.

"We'll keep it simple," he concluded. "Sugar cookies and ice cream for dessert." He tilted his head toward the pantry. "Check the freezer and see what kind of ice cream we've got."

In the face of his domineering attitude, her reminders to herself for calmness dissipated to the four winds. "We? See what kind of ice cream *we've* got?" Angry color washed into Annie's cheeks. Stubbornness and self-preservation urged her to do what she'd promised herself she wouldn't. She clapped her hands onto her hips and stuck out her chin. "I'll be darned if I'm going to take orders from you right here in my own kitchen."

"Whatever you say, boss lady," he answered, slamming the recipe binder shut. "You're obviously more interested in being in control than taking care of your guests. No wonder this place is losing money like water down a sinkhole."

Annie's breath drew in sharply. How did he know that? She had kept it a strict secret. Too angry to confirm or deny it, she merely glared at him until he turned and started from the room. When she saw that he was really leaving, her common sense finally kicked in.

"Wait, Flynn!"

He stopped with one hand on the swinging door and glanced over his shoulder at her. "Yes?"

Annie cleared her throat. "I'm . . . I'm sorry. I would be glad for your help. I can't do this alone." Noting the skeptical lift of his brow, she amended, "Well, all right. I can't do this at all, but this is my inn and I'm not used to taking orders from anyone else."

"Get used to it—at least for today," he advised, strolling to the counter. "Now, check on that ice cream."

Annie headed for the pantry, grousing, "Were you this bossy when we were married?"

"We're still married," he said pointedly, reaching for a large mixing bowl and an egg whisk suspended from a hook over the work island.

"You know what I mean."

"Of course I was. I've always been this bossy."

She walked into the nearby pantry, lifted the lid of the big freezer and stood, peering inside. "How on earth did I stand it?"

"I never heard any complaints from you," he answered. "But, then, you weren't this stubborn before."

"This is the real me," she reminded him defiantly.

She heard him mumbling under his breath, probably mourning the loss of the quiet, malleable girl she'd apparently been before.

"When I got too overbearing, you would give me a sweet, gentle smile," he answered. "And I would forget all about being the boss and take you into the bedroom where I would make sweet, gentle love to you. Care to try that method?"

"No!" Annie choked out. Heat—not from anger this time—flooded her veins. She grabbed the nearest thing she saw, a packet of green peas, and held it to her cheek. His words brought vivid pictures to her mind. Who needed memories of two years ago when she had his explicit words and the memory of his kiss an hour ago?

No doubt he said such things to unnerve her, to keep the upper hand in this crazy tug-of-war. He was trying to determine if she was really telling him the truth. She had to deny him the satisfaction of seeing her react. If she could remain calm and in control, this matter could be worked out the way she wanted—which was to have Flynn Parker go back to his own life and let her get on with hers.

The secret was to keep Flynn out of her life at the inn, to make sure he didn't know her very well, nor she him. And she would do that, too, as soon as she no longer needed his help. With a despairing groan at her hypocrisy, she shifted the bag of peas to her forehead.

In the meantime, she wasn't going to allow a repeat of that kiss. She was determined to hang on to her sanity and her common sense.

With a decisive nod, Annie dropped the packet of peas into the freezer, made note of the variety of ice cream inside and closed the lid.

That was it, she assured herself. All that needed to be done was to send Flynn back to his own life—without her.

"There's praline, rocky road, vanilla and…" Her voice trailed off when she saw that Flynn was no longer alone. Beatrice and Velma stood by the counter, obviously fascinated by the sight of him blending butter and sugar and beating in eggs. Both women were smiling and chatting while Flynn listened with an interested expression on his face.

Annie had to admit that there was something very appealing about someone so masculine showing competence in the kitchen. He had forgone the powerful industrial mixer Mary always used. Instead, he had the large, stainless steel mixing bowl cradled in the crook of his elbow. The muscles in his hand and forearm bunched and flexed as he whipped the egg whisk around in a blur of motion, turning the mixture into a creamy mass in no time.

Velma and Beatrice watched the action with as much fascination as Annie did. Flynn glanced up and smiled at something the waitress said. Velma, gray-haired and approaching retirement, returned the smile, seeming to drop ten years in an instant.

From nowhere, jealousy lashed at Annie, taking her by surprise. He never smiled at *her* like that, and she was supposed to be his wife! Of course, he didn't believe that she couldn't remember being his wife, and she wasn't sure she believed he was really her husband. So why the jealousy? How could she be jealous over someone she wanted out of her life? Someone she didn't remember and didn't love?

Confused and distraught over her contradictory feelings, Annie continued into the kitchen where she murmured a greeting to her employees and made her ice-cream report to Flynn. Under his watchful direction, she began preparing vegetables for the soup while Beatrice returned to her housekeeping chores and Velma covered the front desk.

They also pitched in to help with lunch preparations. With Flynn in command, and with the cooperation of his three women assistants, things went smoothly for lunch and dinner. Annie explained their situation to the inn's guests, who, as Flynn had predicted, were understanding—even the demanding triplets.

In the moments when they were alone, Flynn tried to draw Annie into conversation, but she was subdued, feeling again the weight of emotional pressures she had thought were resolved. She was reconciled to the deaths of her parents, had even come to terms with her loss of memory. She had been sure she would never recall those lost weeks in Seattle, convincing herself nothing had happened during that time that could be significant in her present or future.

She had been wrong, though, and now her heart seemed to be trying to remember what her mind couldn't.

By eight o'clock that evening, Velma and Beatrice had shepherded the guests out of the dining room for the evening's entertainment. Flynn began putting up the chairs and vacuuming the carpet, only to be interrupted by Mrs Grindle, who twittered in to congratulate him on the fine meal. Mrs Shaw and Mrs Bennett were hot on her heels.

The poor man looked stunned at being accosted by three ladies who dressed themselves in clothing styles forty years too young for them and loaded themselves down with thousands of dollars worth of jewelry.

Annie couldn't help grinning at Flynn's expression when the ladies crowded in close, trapping him. His only way out was under a table or over the buffet. He could have made an escape but politeness kept him from trying it.

He cast Annie a look that begged for rescue, but she only smiled serenely and wiggled her fingers at him, then rubbed her hands together gleefully. Oh, she was enjoying this.

Mrs Grindle patted her bright red hair and fluttered her false eyelashes shamelessly. "Mary tries, of course, the dear girl, but everyone knows it takes a real man to be a great chef." She gave his sinewy forearms a frankly appreciative look.

Not to be outdone, her sisters elbowed her aside. "Mabel is right, although I hate to admit it. There's nothing like a real man in the kitchen." Mrs Shaw treated him to a coquettish little wrinkle of the nose, and Mrs Bennett reached up and tweaked his ear.

Over the tops of the ladies' heads, Flynn gave Annie a look that changed from alarmed to frankly horrified. Annie leaned on her broom and answered him with a simpering smile that matched that of his admirers.

"A real man in the kitchen, and everywhere else," Mrs Bennett said. "We were so surprised to learn that you're helping out here. Don't your own hotels keep you busy enough?"

"Yes, but..."

"Maybe you're thinking of buying this one."

For some reason, Flynn's gaze shot to Annie, but Mrs Shaw quickly drew his attention by stepping neatly in front of Mrs Bennett. "Don't be silly, Mildred. Why would he want a little place like this?"

"Well, it was just a thought." Mrs Bennett shoved at her sister. "Move over, Mavis, I need to talk to Mr Parker." Mavis made a disgruntled squeak as she stumbled out of the way.

Puffed up with self-importance, Mrs Bennett tugged at the hem of her sequined cocktail jacket and said, "Please call me Mildred. After all, we don't need to be too formal. I know your mother." She said it in a tone that hinted the two of them got together every week for coffee and gossip. She gave her sisters a look that clearly said, "Ha! Top that!"

"You know my mother?" Flynn asked. "I don't think she's ever mentioned you."

Mabel and Mavis snickered, but Mildred went on undeterred. "It's true. We worked together on a charity auction last year."

"Did you?"

"Oh, Mildred," Mabel broke in. "He doesn't want to hear about that."

Annie couldn't resist. "Oh, yes, he does." She propped her broom against the wall and stepped forward. "He would love to hear about it." She winked at Flynn's murderous glare.

Mildred nodded in triumph. "Since your mother and I are friends, I know you'll be happy to come join us for dancing this evening. I need a dancing partner."

"So do I."

"So do I."

A reddish stain washed over Flynn's face. Annie watched him with delight. Who would have thought the president and CEO of Parker Hotels could be disconcerted by three society women? The prospect of doing triple duty on the dance floor didn't appeal to him.

"I'm afraid I can't tonight..."

"Of course you can," Annie piped up. "You can't disappoint our guests. That's not something a *real* man would do."

Flynn answered her with a black stare, but directed his words to Mildred. "I'll be happy to, ma'am."

"Oh, wonderful," Mildred gushed, turning toward the door. "I'll go tell Beatrice and Velma to get everything ready."

"No, I will," Mavis shouted, darting after her.

"No, me," Mabel insisted, joining the chase.

The three of them created a logjam at the doorway as they tried to get through at the same time. Finally, with much grunting and shoving, they popped through like a cork out of a bottle and rushed to the common room.

Laughing, Annie turned to pick up her broom and finish sweeping.

Flynn plucked it out of her hand. "I've just seen a side to your personality I never would have expected, Anne Christina. That was low. Very low."

Annie's eyes brimmed with laughter and it bubbled in her voice. "Nonsense. I was only allowing you to uphold the Parker Hotel motto. Doesn't it say, 'Get some rest. We'll take care of everything'? Think how well those ladies will rest after a little gentle exercise on the dance floor. A few stately waltzes, a sedate two-step and they'll head right off for slumberland."

He frowned and squinted at her. "How come I'm not buying this?"

Her shrug was as pure and innocent as fresh snow. "I don't know, Flynn. Maybe you're a skeptic. Trust me, I know these ladies. They've been coming here since I was a little girl." She pulled the broom away from him, preparing to finish her job.

"Oh, no, you don't." Flynn laid a hand on her shoulder and removed the broom from her grip with the other. "If I dance, you do, too. You got me into this."

"I just wanted to help out a real man like you," she insisted as he hustled her toward the common room.

"Keep it up, Annie, just keep it up," he said mildly, but with a hint of deviltry in his face. "You'll find out what a real man I am, and this time, you won't forget."

That threat sounded more like a promise. Annie reacted with a ripple of pleasure that ran from her hand to her shoulder. She hoped Flynn didn't notice.

When they reached the common room, the triplets were waiting for him. Since dancing had been her idea, Mildred was first in line.

She popped a tape into the stereo and tangoed her way over to Flynn, the short, frilly hem of her black chiffon skirt swirling around her chubby knees.

"Stately waltz?" Flynn muttered under his breath. "Sedate two-step? I'll get you for this, Annie. I promise."

Annie swallowed a laugh as Mildred hustled him away. He was hard-pressed to keep up with the energetic lady, but Annie admired his efforts.

She settled on a sofa and lifted her feet onto a hassock, glad to rest them for a while. Flynn got no rest at all. Mildred may have liked the tango, but Mabel enjoyed the cha-cha and Mavis preferred the foxtrot. Annie had to admit that there weren't too many young men who could do all three, and certainly not as well as Flynn was doing them.

A few of the other guests came in to join the fun. Annie visited with those who stayed to watch. She waved at Flynn every time he swooped by with Mildred, Mavis or Mabel.

Finally, someone put on a tape of slow dance music and the sisters looked around with disgust. "Hmph," Mavis said. "I was going to form a conga line next."

"I suppose we'll have to do that tomorrow night," Mabel answered. "Thanks for the dance, Flynn, honey," she said. "We hate to disappoint you, but this isn't our kind of music. If we wanted to *crawl* around the dance floor, we would have brought our own husbands to dance with." To her sisters, she said, "Let's go see if we can challenge anyone to a moonlight run on the beach."

"My pleasure, ladies," he said with a gallant salute, but discovered he was talking to their retreating backs as they scuttled toward the door.

Annie had to give him credit for not groaning in relief until after they had rushed out.

She stood and walked over to him, her blue eyes sparkling. "Thank you for making the guests happy." She choked with laughter. "It was absolutely... unforgettable. Do you want to collapse now? I'm certified in CPR and... Oh!''

Flynn's hands had shot out and swept her into his arms. "I'll show you who needs CPR," he promised.

Before she could catch her breath, he had wrapped his arms around her, pulled her against his body and urged her to follow his lead.

After a few stumbling missteps, Annie caught up with him, then matched her steps to his. Once they hit their rhythm, the dance was flawless. Annie blinked at him. She had never been able to dance so well and gracefully with someone so much taller, but with Flynn, it was effortless. Again, she wondered if her body was remembering what her mind couldn't.

"That was a good one, Annie.''

Her blue eyes could have been patented for their innocence. "Why, what do you mean, Flynn?"

"Conning me into thinking those three dynamos were ready to nod off any second. You're a clever woman.''

"I know," she said with fake modesty. "I try to be humble about it, though.''

His chuckle rumbled up through his chest. Annie looked at him, listening with pleasure to that delightfully natural sound, the first she'd heard from him. Happiness flooded through her, bringing warmth and desire. She thrilled to the feel of her small hand tucked into his, to his hand, strong and steady, against the small of her back.

Being close to him brought sheer pleasure and joy, but not a little sorrow. How could she have forgotten this? Why would her mind have blocked out something this wonderful? Because she had no answer, she concentrated on the music and the direction her feet were going, living only in the moment.

Although she told herself it probably wasn't a good idea to let down her guard, Annie relaxed in his arms. The evening had been such a pleasant break from the turmoil she'd known for two days. She had managed to find time for a nap that afternoon, but as the tension relaxed, she began to realize how exhausted she was. A mild headache was beginning to pound in her temples.

Valiantly, she fought the desire to lay her head against his solid strength and whimper. Even though she had clearly told him she was the one responsible for the inn, it was wonderful to relax for a few minutes and escape from her duties. For an instant, she fantasized about letting him carry all of her burdens. It was too tempting, so she pulled away when the music ended. Looking around, she discovered that they were alone. Apparently, several people had been interested in a moonlight run with the triplets. Annie hadn't even noticed when they'd left. Some innkeeper she was, not even noticing when her guests had departed. Obviously, it was high time she paid attention to something other than Flynn.

Quickly, she stepped back and turned to the stereo system, where she busied herself putting away the music tapes. Once that was done, she started from the room. "Velma will be locking up at eleven. Good night, Flynn."

He took a swift, gliding step to the side and blocked her path. "It's too early for bed. If you go to sleep now, you'll be awake long before dawn."

She almost told him about her sleepless night, but he would guess the reason, so she answered flippantly, "I'll take my chances."

"No. Let's go for a walk."

"Are you kidding? I can barely move, much less walk." She lifted both hands to massage the pain in her head.

"You're getting a headache, aren't you? Starting in your left temple."

Annie froze as her eyes shot up to meet his. "How did you—?"

"That, at least, hasn't changed. It always happens when you get overtired." His eyes had turned dark and fiercely green, and he regarded her with challenge in his eyes. "You need to relax before you try to sleep."

As if that could happen with him around! Back straight, she moved away. "I'll relax in the shower—then I'm going to fall into bed."

He stepped closer but didn't speak again until she looked up, meeting his eyes. "I could rub your neck, your shoulders." His voice had gone low, invitingly seductive, sending a ripple of anticipation across the very areas of her body that he thought needed his attention.

Her voice was strangled as she said, "No."

"Annie, one little neck massage doesn't mean a lifetime commitment—neither does one little kiss."

It hadn't been so little, at least not to her. "I'm sure I don't know what you mean."

"I mean that if you don't stop being so tense, nervous and uncooperative we're never going to get things worked out between us."

CHAPTER FIVE

ANNIE folded her arms. As much as she hated to admit it, she knew he was right, but events were moving so quickly, and each new development was so devastating to her peace of mind, that obstinance was her only defense.

When she didn't answer, he repeated his request. "Go for a walk with me."

Annie's hands dropped limply to her sides and the fight drained out of her. "Don't you know when to quit?"

The corner of his mouth lifted. He raised his arm and used his sleeve to blot perspiration from his forehead. It left his jet-black hair tousled and falling over his forehead. "Never given it a try. I'll let you know what happens if I ever do. Let's go for a walk. You owe me for throwing me to Mrs Grumble and her sisters."

"That's *Grindle*," Annie corrected. "You really impressed them. They've been coming here every year since I can remember and nothing has ever pleased them."

"Except my cooking."

Despite her exhaustion, her eyes laughed at him. "And your dancing. I had no idea that any man under fifty knew all those dances."

His face softened. "My mother and my sister's doing, especially my sister. She went through a phase in junior high when she fell in love with old movies and wanted to learn every step that Fred and Ginger ever danced. I was drafted to be her partner.''

"How old were you at the time?''

He rolled his eyes. "Twenty-four. I've always been a sucker for her.''

Looking at him, at the affection in his face, Annie felt her heart begin a slow, steady thudding, awakening parts of her that she had thought were too tired to feel anything. This was a side of him she hadn't seen, that of a family man. It forced her to entertain tender feelings she didn't want. Nevertheless, her grin faded into a trembling smile. "All right. I'll walk with you.''

He nodded as if he'd expected no other answer and said, "I'll get your jacket. Meet me in the foyer.''

While she waited for him to fetch the tan corduroy jacket from her small bedroom, she reached down to tug the sleeves of her sweater into her palms. When he returned and held it out to her, she turned so he could slip the jacket over her arms.

Flynn pulled it up to her shoulders, and while she adjusted the sleeves, he lifted her hair out of the collar. When he didn't drop her hair against her back and move away, Annie went very still. Cautiously, she turned her head and found him holding the bright strands in both his hands.

When he spoke, his voice was low and intimate. "For two years, I've run after every woman with hair this color, thinking it was you.'' He turned his hand, catching the light in the strands, then he looked up to meet her startled gaze. "I was a fool. No one else has hair this color."

Hair had no nerves, no feeling. Annie knew that, and yet she could feel an electric shock travel up the shafts and tingle across her scalp. Disconcerted, she reached out to ease it from his grasp, then slipped away from him.

Flynn let his hands drop to his sides, then he squared his shoulders. "Shall we go?"

Grateful for the break in the tension, Annie swung away from him, energized by nervousness. She tried for nonchalance as she asked, "Where shall we walk?"

"The three dancing grannies are on the beach," he said, holding the door for her. "Let's go in the other direction."

"The path to the gardens is lighted. We can go there."

They walked in silence for several minutes. Annie breathed deeply of the salt air, realizing that Flynn had been right again. She had needed time to relax and wind down before trying to sleep, even though most of her tension was caused by the man beside her.

Her reactions to him were wildly askew. She had to get them under control, but first she needed to bring her thoughts about him into order and she needed answers to the many questions that still troubled her.

She cast him a sidelong glance, trying to decipher the enigma of Flynn Parker. He was accustomed to power, to giving orders and having people leap to follow those orders. He could have called

up one of his hotels and had a chef flown in by jet
to handle the relatively small needs of the
Anapamua Island Inn, but that hadn't seemed to
occur to him. Instead, he'd done it himself.

Deep in thought, Annie hadn't noticed where
they were walking until Flynn skirted the gardens
and started up the path to the landing strip.

"Uh, Flynn," she said, skidding to a stop. "Why
don't we just go around the garden a few more
times? Nothing there to trip us up."

He turned to face her, his dark brows drawing
together in a straight line. "The lane up to the
landing strip is lighted, too, and it's wider. Why
don't we—?"

"I don't want to," she snapped, then softened
her tone. "I thought we were walking to relax, not
going for a hike."

"That's not what's bothering you. What's wrong,
Annie?"

She lifted her head, up and away from him.
Sudden tears sprang into her eyes and she blinked
them back. "I haven't been up there to the airstrip
or to the east end of the island since..."

"Since your parents crashed."

Tears choked her throat, and she cleared them
away. "Ye-yes."

"You haven't been up there at all, not even
once?"

"No."

Regret rolled through her, with sorrow chasing
close behind. She pressed her hands flat against
her stomach.

"You've got to face it sometime." His voice was gruff, almost angry.

"Not tonight."

She swallowed the tears and took a deep breath, exhaling in a long sigh. She wished she could keep herself from showing so much weakness before him. For a moment, she thought he was going to push her into going to the landing strip, after all, but when he answered, his voice was quiet.

"That was a terrible thing for you to have witnessed . . ."

She tried to look into his eyes, darker than ever in the evening gloom, their deepness unrelieved by the dim lanterns above their heads. "Yes, it was. The loss was total and left such a void . . ." She looked at him apologetically. "I must seem like such a coward to you. I mean, you lost your father, too."

"I didn't see it happen." His voice was raw and raspy. "But I did walk into his office a few days later. It looked as if he'd stepped out for just a minute, to speak to someone down the hall, maybe. His pen was on top of a pile of papers. His coffee cup was half full. His secretary, who'd been with him for thirty years, couldn't bear to go in and clear it away."

Annie ached to put her arms around him and hold him, but how would he take it—this stranger she had married?

After a moment, Flynn cleared his throat. "I don't understand why you didn't tell me about it, about what you'd been through."

There it was again—Flynn's inability or refusal to believe she was telling the truth. Her sympathy disappeared and her fingers curled tensely into her palms. "I can't answer that because I don't remember."

"Is it possible that you choose not to remember?"

"No. Why would I want to do that?"

"Because you married me, but you didn't trust me." His words were flat, without inflection.

Annie stared to protest, but stopped herself. How could she deny it? She didn't know if it was true, but she didn't like what he was implying about her. "*If* I married you, I must have trusted you."

"If you'd trusted me, you would have told me," he shot back. "The only thing you told me was that your parents had recently died."

Annie's emotions had swung from regret and sorrow to annoyance, but she answered in a level tone. "Maybe my mind blocked it out—not that it had happened, but I must have blocked out the details. The reality."

"What happens if you remember those weeks—remember me?"

She tilted her head and stared at the sky. The clouds that had shrouded the island earlier were beginning to break up, and stars appeared as if springing to life in the velvety darkness. "If that happens, I'll deal with it." She started down the path to the inn, drawn by the inviting warmth of the lights.

"*We'll* deal with it," he bit out, and she looked around quickly to see the determination in his eyes.

Annie shivered and kept walking. She didn't like the claim he had on her. "Please try to remember that before yesterday I knew nothing about you."

Flynn fell into step beside her and held his hands out at his sides, palm up. "What do you want to know? Now's your chance to ask."

"I want to know the answer to the question I tried to ask you last night. I want to know what I was like—what my personality was like when we met. You said I was quiet, controlled."

"Unlike you are now. You were reserved. Sad. Now I know why."

Annie wondered yet again what he could have found attractive about her. He didn't seem like the type of man to be interested in a clinging woman or one steeped in self-pity. "Where did we meet?"

"Heritage Inns had a grand opening of the new hotel where you worked. I went to see what the competition was up to. You were there."

He stopped, leaving Annie unsatisfied with his explanation. "And?"

"We talked. We dated. We married."

"In two weeks?" She snorted. "Must have been some talks and some dates." There was more to it than that, she knew. To someone who was emotionally distraught, his strength and air of command would have been very attractive.

As they neared the inn, Annie could read his expression in the glow from the lights coming through the windows. He looked irritated at her probing. "They were…strange talks. You told me very little about yourself except, as I told you, to say that your parents had recently died. I didn't even know it had happened in a plane crash, although whenever you heard one . . ."

"What?"

His eyes locked with hers. "You seemed to panic. The only place you felt safe was in my arms."

The memory of being in his arms earlier that day rushed through her and she spun away from him. She could see how easy it would be to depend on him for refuge, and yet something about the way he said it made her certain that he had done much more than merely hold her and kiss her as he had that morning.

It was unnerving to realize that this stranger knew every inch of her body and yet she knew nothing of him. Unconsciously, her hand covered the scar on her elbow, received in a fall from a bicycle when she was ten. It was small, not easily noticed by a casual observer, but it was the type of thing a lover would have seen.

By now, they had reached the terrace and climbed the wide, shallow steps together. "Didn't you wonder why I wouldn't tell you? Did you see me as some sort of woman of mystery?"

"It's like I said, Annie, I hoped you would confide in me when you trusted me." Flynn stopped on the flagstone terrace. In the soft lighting, he looked big, dark and dangerous. "How was I to know you would disappear before that happened?"

Annie felt embarrassed, ashamed of her actions, although she certainly hadn't been herself when she had left him. "I can understand your feelings. You must have felt betrayed."

"You'd made a fool of me. I was mad as hell."

"I can see why. I won't fight it when you do file for divorce and I certainly don't expect any kind of spousal support, after all— What's the matter?"

He was looking at her as if she was hallucinating. "What makes you think I intend to divorce you?"

Annie gaped at him. "Why wouldn't you want a divorce? It's not as though I'm really the person you married."

"I thought we'd established this already," Flynn said impatiently. "Why rush into a divorce? It's been two years. What's the hurry? You're not even convinced we're really married."

"You're not convinced that I've really forgotten you—being married to you."

"Then those are the two issues we need to focus on, aren't they?"

Annie scowled at him. "Then let's do that. When can I expect to see our marriage certificate—if it really exists?"

"My secretary is bringing it in person tomorrow," he answered in a tone that matched hers for belligerence. "When can I expect proof of your memory loss?"

She straightened and her arms drifted to her sides. "What do you mean?"

"I want to talk to your doctor."

"What on earth for?"

"You want proof, don't you? Well, so do I."

Annie almost refused, but then reconsidered. It was only fair that Flynn talk to Dr Landerson. Then the matter would be settled. "I'll call his office as soon as it opens in the morning. Then we'll both have the answers we want and we can decide what needs to be done.''

Flynn didn't answer right away. He covered the bottom half of his face with his hand, the long fingers digging into the hollows of his cheeks as he considered her. After a silent minute, he said, ''I don't think I have to guess what you'll want us to do.''

''I want a resolution to this.''

''Meaning a divorce.''

''That's right. Why not?'' She threw her hands wide. ''This is my home. My work—my life— everything that's important to me is here. I don't understand why you think I'd want to leave this.''

''You were willing to leave it before.''

''What—? When?''

''You married me with the full knowledge that my life, *my* work was in San Francisco, that I was only in Seattle for a few months to oversee the renovations to the Parker Hotel Seattle. You never said anything about your life here, the inn or much of anything else, for that matter.''

Annie pointed a furious finger at his chest. ''See? That proves right there that I wasn't in my right mind. I never want to leave here.''

Flynn stepped closer and leaned down until they were almost nose to nose. His eyes narrowed and his words were slow and distinct. ''Is that because, as you say, your life is here, or because since I came back into your life, you refuse to face up to your responsibilities?''

''Refuse to...'' Her words dried up in a blast of anger. She opened and closed her mouth a couple of times. "My responsibilities are here," she finally choked out. "And furthermore, you have no right—"

"I've got a marriage certificate that says I've got a whole fistful of rights, Annie." Flynn stepped back suddenly. "Maybe you'd better go to bed before I start claiming them. We shouldn't even be discussing this now. You're too tired to be reasonable—or logical. Sleep in tomorrow morning. You need the rest. Velma and I can take care of breakfast."

"Now wait a minute," she began, but he shook his head.

"That's enough. Go to bed."

Even though she sputtered and fumed, he wouldn't listen to another word. She had quickly come to know the stubborn set of his jaw. He held the door open for her, gave her a mocking good-night salute, waving her toward her room and waiting until she actually started in that direction.

Turning, she marched through the door, across the lobby and down the back hall to the kitchen and her bedroom beyond. Annie barely kept herself from slamming her door as she stomped inside. With her back stiff, her eyes full of fury and her steps hard enough to pummel holes in the floor, she paced back and forth across the room.

Oh, he was overbearing. She couldn't imagine why she had married him. He wasn't at all the kind, considerate man she'd always dreamed she would marry—more proof that she hadn't been in her right mind when they'd met.

When she had calmed a bit, she sat down on the side of her bed and tried to decide what it was about Flynn Parker that pushed her into rash statements and furious actions.

It was his take-charge attitude, she decided, along with his ingrained belief that he was right. In a calmer moment, Annie might have acknowledged that he had proven right about several things already. If it hadn't been for him taking over in the kitchen, all the guests would have either checked out of the inn because there was no food or rushed to have their stomachs pumped because she had tried to cook.

Annie took a deep breath and held it for a few seconds, then exhaled slowly. He was so strong and sure of himself. Things seemed to come so easily for him.

She knew what needed to be done, for the inn and the guests, but achieving it was such a struggle.

The inn was hers. She was the third generation of her family who had owned it, and yet she had a horrible fear that she wouldn't be able to make a go of it. She worked so hard to keep the bills and the employees paid, attract new guests, make people comfortable, keep things running smoothly, but financial ruin loomed before her like the mouth of a cavern. Flynn seemed to see the problems at the inn, though he surely didn't know how desperate matters would be if the summer season wasn't profitable.

Annie rubbed her temples. Her father had been much more adept at making the inn pay. He'd even managed to send enough money to Vernon to keep her spendthrift uncle reasonably content. Too bad she hadn't inherited the knack.

Thinking of Vernon and the way her father had handled him brought on a wave of loneliness. She looked around at the room. All of the furniture, from the mahogany headboard she had affixed to her waterbed to the gateleg table and cherry wood chairs by the window, had belonged to her parents. The three of them had shared a small apartment on the top floor of the inn. Annie's mother, Christina, had made it a cozy, inviting place and they had spent wonderful hours together there.

Annie closed her eyes, remembering their times together. Her father, Jason, had loved popcorn so she and her mother had made it for him every night. Annie still couldn't smell it without thinking of him. She had been unable to live in the apartment after she had returned from Seattle, so James and Mary had helped her move her things to this small room. It was her haven, but it wasn't really a home.

She opened her eyes to gaze on the photograph that stood on the nightstand. She picked it up and studied the faces of her parents. If they were here, they could tell her what to do about the inn, and especially about Flynn Parker. Another wave of loneliness hit her. Tears stung her nose and the backs of her eyes, but she pressed her lips together and refused to let them fall. She had shed enough tears already and tears wouldn't help now. Flynn Parker wasn't the type of man who would be swayed by them. Action was the only thing he understood.

It couldn't be true that she had married him knowing she could never return to live on

Anapamua Island. Since her panicked flight from Seattle, the focus of her life had been to make the inn a success. In a way, it was a tribute to her parents.

Returning the photograph to its place, she lay down on her side facing the door and set the waterbed mattress into motion with a kick. Her eyes drifted shut as she rode the gentle wave. It couldn't be true. She wouldn't have voluntarily lived away from the island. Flynn was wrong.

She was floating in clouds, surrounded by warmth and light. She knew she was asleep and didn't want to wake up. It was so pleasant to lie very still, feeling the gentle pitch and roll of the clouds. Someone was holding her hand. She tightened her grip and was rewarded with an answering grasp and a soft chuckle. Something cool and hard was slipped over her finger, then her hand was surrounded again by warmth.

"Annie, love, wake up," a voice said softly. "It's almost noon."

She frowned and mumbled, "Not yet." She wasn't ready to open her eyes. It was too pleasant to float along, holding on to the secure touch.

Annie lifted the warmth to her face and rubbed it against her skin. It was a hand, much bigger than her own, and the back was lightly dusted with springy hairs. Dad? No, it didn't smell or feel like him, but she knew it was a man. Somewhere deep in her mind, memory stirred.

In an effort to strengthen the memory, she pressed her lips to the back of that hand. She was rewarded with a sharp intake of breath, but it hadn't come. from her. Curious, she nuzzled, hoping to hear that sound again.

If she could pinpoint that scent, that touch, that sound, she knew she would be happier than she had been in a long time, but what was it? Who was it? The harder she tried to grasp the memory, the more quickly it faded, then disappeared altogether.

Disappointed, she sighed, and her eyelids opened to see Flynn Parker sitting on the edge of her bed. He was wearing jeans and a red and blue striped polo shirt. His midnight hair was tousled as if he'd been walking in the wind. One corner of his mouth was lifted in a soft smile, his eyes full of something she'd never seen there before. Could it be tenderness?

To her shock, she realized it was his hand she was holding—and kissing! Her fingers sprang away from his and she shot to a sitting position, sending the bed into a surging wave.

She scrambled for the sheet, only to realize that she'd fallen asleep in her trousers and sweater. Self-consciously, she smoothed her hair, then gave him a haughty look. "What are you doing in my room? How did you get in here?"

The expression in his eyes cooled faster than lava hitting an ice floe. "Good morning to you, too, Annie. I came in through the door, which you considerately left unlocked."

"Well, that didn't mean you could just walk right in," she insisted. "The guests are never allowed in here."

"Surely husbands have privileges the guests aren't allowed." His eyebrows lifted slowly. "Why don't you save the outrage for a moment when you don't look like a sleepy kitten, Annie? Funny, I don't remember you being this surly in the mornings."

"I guess that proves that your memory is as flawed as mine, doesn't it?" She lifted her left hand to point him toward the door. A sparkle of light riveted her attention onto the third finger. "What . . . what is that?"

"Your wedding band," he answered calmly as he pulled a folded piece of paper from his breast pocket. "My secretary had some papers for me to sign, so she decided to come in person with them, and our marriage license." He opened the paper and spread it on the white goose-down comforter. "I also asked her to bring your ring."

Annie's mouth dropped open as she stared at it, winking and sparkling in the morning light. "Ring or rink? Pairs of figure skaters could do routines on this thing. This diamond is at least two carats. And these . . . are these sapphires?" Three of them marched down the gold band on each side of the central stone.

"Actually the diamond is four carats," he said, and his lips twitched. "That's one thing that hasn't changed about you. You thought it was too showy before, too."

"I'm glad to know I didn't lose all my senses," she murmured, and reached to take it off.

His fingers closed over hers and she felt again the security of his touch. "Keep it on for a minute,"

he said. "Who knows? You may grow to like it."
With his other hand, he lifted the marriage license
and held it up for her to read.

"See? Here's the proof that you have a right to
wear that ring."

Annie skimmed the document, then reached out
to hold it and read it again more carefully. All the
words were there, stating that Anne Christina Locke
had indeed married Flynn MacHugh Parker in
February two years ago. She might still have fought
the truth of the document if her own signature
hadn't been staring back at her from the page.
There was no mistaking the sharply angled A and
looping capital L with which she always wrote her
name.

Color drained from her face and she lifted tor-
mented eyes to him. "It's really true, then," she
whispered. "I'm really married to you, but I don't
remember where we married, or when."

The expression drained from Flynn's dark green
eyes, leaving them blank. "And obviously you don't
remember why, either."

Annie looked away from him, staring at the
bright sunlight shining through the lace-paneled
curtains. Deep in her heart she had known he was
telling the truth. She just hadn't been able to admit
it. "Now...now I suppose we have to decide what
to do about it."

Flynn stood abruptly. "Like I said last night, we
already know what you want to do about it, Annie.
But my questions still haven't been answered."

Annie shoved aside her momentary shock, scooted to the edge of the bed and stood to face him. "I'll call my doctor right away and see when we can get in to see him. He'll be able to answer all your questions."

Flynn's gaze sharpened as it roved over her sleep-tangled hair and her anxious face. "Maybe not all of them," he said quietly.

Annie clasped her hands in front of her, unsure and ill at ease. "I . . . I have to shower and change. I'm sure there's lots to do."

Flynn turned away. "Less than you'd like to think, Annie. James has recovered and is in the kitchen. Everything's running smoothly."

"Good," she said to his retreating back. "That's the way I like it."

"I'll be up in my suite going over some contracts with my secretary."

"Good, you can do your own work for a while, and let me do mine."

He didn't answer, and she couldn't figure out how the set of someone's shoulders could look so smug.

Annie showered and dressed quickly in khaki trousers and a pumpkin-colored shirt. The first thing she did was drop the flashy ring into the pocket, then hurried in to check on things in the kitchen and dining room. As Flynn had said, James was handling things with the help of Beatrice and Velma. He waved away her offer of help, and she headed into the office. She placed the ring in a small box of keepsakes inside the safe, closed the door securely and called her doctor.

After making an appointment for the next day, she called Carlos on the walkie-talkie and said she would need the cabin cruiser readied for a trip to Santa Barbara. It would be a slower method of travel than Flynn was probably accustomed to, but she wouldn't fly. Fortunately, he seemed to know that, so she didn't anticipate an argument.

She was settling down to some paperwork when the phone rang. Answering it, she was dismayed to hear her uncle Vernon's voice.

He didn't bother to ask about her health or anything else, but plunged right in. "Annie, I need—"

"Money," she interrupted sardonically. Leaning back in her worn desk chair, she prepared for their usual argument. "Hello, Vernon, so what else is new?"

"Don't get sarcastic with me, young lady," he said testily. "I'm part owner of that place and I have a right to a share in the profits."

"I don't see why, since you don't share in the work." Here, or anywhere else. He had held any number of jobs, which he quit when he had enough money to indulge his real profession—gambling. When he ran out of funds, he called on her.

"Don't forget, dear niece, that my father left me more than half of that business."

It was true, and it was a sore point with Annie. In the hopes that Vernon would straighten out and take an interest in the inn, Annie's grandfather had left him the major share of the business. The old man had been a bit of a chauvinist, unwilling to consider that his daughter, Christina, could do a better job of running the place in partnership with her husband.

"Well, then," she said, cheerfully. "Why don't you come on over and do more than half the work? I'd be glad to have your help."

"I will come over, and soon, Annie. I've got a big plan for the place, and like it or not, you'll go along with it."

"Uh-huh, sure, Vernon. Is this anything like the ballroom you wanted us to add on last year?"

The notion had been ridiculous, and they both knew it. He knew nothing about operating the inn and cared less than nothing about learning.

"I'll be over soon, Annie, and we'll talk. It's time some changes were made." He hung up before she could respond and she cradled the phone with an expression of disgust. Little did he know that she was already in the middle of a big change in her life. Much bigger than anything he could imagine.

CHAPTER SIX

"Now we both know everything we need to know," Annie said, folding her hands carefully around a mug of coffee.

"At least about this amnesia of yours," Flynn responded. "There are still other questions."

Mary had recovered from the flu and returned to work, so Annie and Flynn had come to Santa Barbara for the day. Now that their talk with the doctor was over, Flynn had brought her to have lunch in a nearby restaurant. Neither of them was hungry, though. She had only picked at her salad, and he had eaten less than half of his sandwich.

"You know that my memory loss is probably permanent."

"That's what he said," Flynn agreed. "'Doubtless permanent and irreparable.' Now we've got to decide how we're going to deal with it."

"Deal with it? Why, you go your way, and I go mine, obviously. We have separate careers, separate lives."

"We have a marriage license."

She certainly couldn't dispute that. She'd seen it herself.

"Annie, aren't you the least bit curious about why we got married after only knowing each other two weeks?"

She blinked at him and color flushed beneath her skin, pinkening her soft, fair face. She *knew* why they'd married. Sexual attraction.

She cleared her throat softly and looked away. The large dining room was full of people, none of whom were paying any attention whatsoever to them, but she felt as if all eyes were on them. She couldn't deny that she was attracted to him, that her body knew more than her mind did. No doubt, that had been the case two years ago, also.

"Annie?" he prompted.

"Of course I am. I've asked you..."

"You asked about the facts. I'm wondering if you're curious about the attraction between us."

"Certainly, I think we were very attracted to each other, although..." She cast him a puzzled look. "After having seen that photograph of myself, and the one of us together, I can't help wondering what you found attractive about me. I looked as if I was in shock."

Amusement lightened Flynn's expression. "I'll admit you were much quieter then than you are now. Less argumentative, too."

"Easily led, you mean." She placed her elbow on the table and plopped her chin into her palm as she looked at him. He had said she was gentle and sweet, a description that could have made her laugh if she'd been in the mood to do so. She had always been outspoken and brash, often acting before thinking. She couldn't imagine herself as he described her.

"What do you have in mind, Flynn? That we can start all over again? We may discover that we can't stand each other."

He lifted one shoulder in a shrug. "Maybe. As you say, you're not the same person. Well, neither am I." His eyes drifted over her in lazy possessiveness, and she knew that wasn't what he was thinking. Fingers of apprehension and excitement seemed to be stroking over her spine, sending shivers of awareness through her.

"Annie, I have four days of my vacation left. I'm not going to waste them chasing you all over Anapamua Island, begging for your attention. We're married, and even though we've been separated for two years, our marriage is still valid. I don't intend to seek a divorce, and I don't intend to let you file for one, either. At least, not yet," he said in a tone that invited no argument.

She argued anyway. "You can't make that decision for me."

"I have every right to," he said, sitting forward suddenly, his expression intent. "If you'll listen for a minute without interrupting, I'll explain."

Annie spread her hands on the tabletop, trying to appear reasonable. "Explain away."

"We need to start all over again. Get to know each other again. As you've said several times, you're not the same person I met in Seattle. Well, I've changed, too, but one thing about me hasn't changed. I don't give up easily."

"No kidding," she sighed, earning a scowl from him.

"There was something between us before, and deny it if you want, there still is."

Annie drew her bottom lip beneath her front teeth as she remembered the scene in her bedroom yesterday morning. She couldn't deny the attraction between them. It was as real as Flynn's determination to pursue it.

"I don't deny it," she said. "But I don't see where it could possibly lead. There are too many differences between us, and don't you think we're trying to build on something that may not exist?"

"How will we know for sure if we don't try?" he challenged. "You don't strike me as a coward."

"I'm not!"

"Then why not find out where this leads? We'll be together, do things together, talk the way we used to. After all, what harm could be done, in four days?"

It *sounded* perfectly reasonable, like something they both should want. It *sounded* like a way to gain all the information they needed in order to resolve the question of their marriage, but the thought of four days alone with him filled her with a heavy beat of anticipation. Still, Annie found herself looking into the verdant darkness of his eyes and nodding. "All right, Flynn. I'll do it."

"I think you need to take some time off." Annie looked up from the mound of paperwork on her desk. A tiny line appeared between her brows as she frowned at the man standing in the doorway. She would have expected that kind of statement from Flynn, but it was James who ambled in from the reception area and sat in the chair beside the filing cabinet. He stretched his long legs out until they almost reached the door and crossed them at the ankle. Folding his hands, he propped them on his chest, leaned his head against the back of the chair and tilted it so he could look at her.

Annie smiled. No one could relax as quickly as James could. Maybe she should have him teach the technique to Flynn. She had yet to see him simply relax and do nothing.

Realizing that she was thinking like a wife, she tossed the letter opener down on the pile of mail she and Flynn had picked up in the city the day before, and propped her chin on her hand. "Do you think I should lie low after the bombshell I dropped on the staff this morning?"

James's handsome face creased into a grin. "No, but after my mom recovers from her shock, she might turn you over her knee and paddle you for not telling her about Flynn as soon as he arrived. She's mad at *me* for not telling her."

Annie cringed. "I would have told her if she hadn't been sick, and by the time she was well, things were moving along—"

"Encouraged by an irresistible force named Flynn Parker. She was suspicious when the two of you went into Santa Barbara together yesterday, but I think she'll forgive you eventually. She agrees with me, though. You need to take some time off. You need to give your full attention to the decision of whether or not to remain married to Flynn."

Although she had told the other staff members the bare facts about her relationship with Flynn,

Annie had revealed the whole story to Mary as she had to James, including her agreement with Flynn that they explore the possibility of remaining married.

Thinking of it, she pressed her hands against the pit of her stomach, which seemed to be trying to hurl itself up into her lungs. Even after twenty-four hours, she still felt ready to hyperventilate at the idea. She hadn't seen Flynn yet that morning, but she knew he would soon appear, and they would begin their four-day trial marriage.

"I suppose you're right," she said slowly. "If you think you can handle the front desk, and—"

"Don't worry about a thing," James said with a wink. "The Marines have landed."

The bell on the front desk sounded with three impatient rings. He sat forward and looked out to see their three most demanding guests standing there, each of them with a hand hovering over the bell. He groaned and rolled his eyes at Annie, who grinned. "See? I'll have the terrible triplets eating out of my hand in no time."

"If they don't snap it off first." Annie watched him go, then stood up and began clearing her desk. Most of the things cluttering it could wait a few days. There was no use worrying over the bills. She couldn't pay them yet, anyway. When a few more guests had come and gone, she could deal with them. She could call some of their creditors and explain the situation. She had found that most people were willing to accept partial payment until she could get caught up.

All except Uncle Vernon. He generally demanded money quickly, and in large amounts. She paused as she sorted the pile of bills. She couldn't help wondering what big plan Vernon had concocted now. His plans usually cost the inn money and almost always led to an argument between them. She regretted that her relationship with her closest relative was so bad, but truly, she didn't think it was her fault. Her greatest fault lay in not putting her foot down with Vernon, not being decisive in refusing to give him money.

Perhaps indecision was more of a problem for her than she had thought.

James was right. The decision she needed to make about Flynn was one that demanded her full attention. Since Flynn's arrival, she had either been fighting the truth about their marriage, or reacting to everything he said or did. It was time for her to act, to be a full partner in this decision, not merely accept whatever he might decide. The thought of remaining married to him filled her with awe and trepidation, but the idea of not doing so filled her with dread. She locked her desk and closed the office door.

As she passed the front desk, Mavis, Mabel and Mildred called out to her. She stopped and smiled at them, congratulating herself for not bursting into laughter.

The three of them were dressed in identical spandex trousers and snug tops in vivid lime green. Annie almost winced when she saw that they carried tennis rackets. Competition between them was so fierce, they usually required first aid afterward.

"Annie, dear, we just heard the news," Mavis gushed. "You and that sexy Mr Parker are married!"

"We couldn't believe it," her sisters chimed in. "Congratulations! You've gotten yourself one fine hunk of a man."

"Great dancer, too," Mildred added with a dreamy look in her eyes. "You're one lucky girl."

Annie didn't know which one of her employees had been spreading the news, but she wished they hadn't. Apparently, though, these ladies thought it was a recent event. She wouldn't have to make any awkward explanations.

"Thank you, I feel lucky," she said, and was pleased to know she was speaking the truth.

"When will you be moving?" Mildred asked.

"Moving?"

"To San Francisco, you silly goose, to the family mansion. Of course, you've seen it, and—"

"No, I haven't."

"Whirlwind courtship." Mabel almost swooned. "Oh, that's so romantic."

"Well, I've seen it," Mildred said, directing a smirk at the other two. "It's just beautiful. Almost as big as this inn. You'll love living there."

"But what will you do with the inn? Is Parker Hotels taking it over?" Mabel broke in.

"Oh, no, of course not," Annie said. "This is my inn, and besides, what would Parker Hotels want with a place as small at this?"

"I'm sure I don't know, dear. It was only a thought. How are you going to have a marriage if you're here and he's in San Francisco?"

"Uh, well . . ."

"We could buy this place," Mavis said on a burst of inspiration. "Do you think we could start a casino here? It's private property, you know. We could declare it a sovereign nation, like those Indian tribes have done."

"That's a great idea," Mabel said, and Mildred agreed. Engrossed in their plan, the three of them headed for the door.

Annie threw a dismayed look at James, who shook his head at her. "Don't panic." He stepped from behind the desk. "You must have expected to deal with this at some point."

"Not yet." She pressed her fingertips against her lips.

"If you're going to be married to him, you'll have to live with him," he said dryly. "Otherwise it's not much of a marriage."

"I know that."

"But first you've got to decide if you love him enough to make it a real marriage."

"But I—" she began, then stopped in confusion. She had almost said that she did love him and was stunned to discover that it was true. She loved him. How had this happened in less than a week?

"What?" James asked. "Hey, are you all right?"

"Yes. I'm fine," she answered in a faint voice, turning away and almost tripping over her own feet. "I'll see you later."

In a daze, she walked out the door and down the steps into the beautiful spring day, barely noticing where she was headed. She stood in the sunshine for a moment, listening to the sound of the surf

and the call of the sea gulls who inhabited the boa
dock.

She loved the island and everything about it, bu
it wasn't a surge of love for her home that fillec
her as she stood in the sun's warmth. It was lov
for Flynn that glowed within her. What she felt wa
a lightness of spirit she hadn't experienced in mor
than two years. She was wise enough to know tha
it had less to do with the beautiful day than it dic
with Flynn Parker and her love for him. To he
surprise, she realized that she was eager to see him
eager to see where a relationship with him woulc
take her. It was such a relief to give herself per
mission to stop fighting him and surrender to th
attraction she could no longer deny. The matter o
where they would live could be worked out. Sh
couldn't expect everything to be her way. The
would compromise. Love made it easy t
compromise.

Thinking Flynn might have decided to try a gam
of golf with some of the other guests, Annie startec
toward the course, but the sound of little-bo
laughter drew her around the end of the building

She found Flynn seated on the ground with Luis
The two of them had a mass of string on the gras
in front of them. They looked as though they'd bee
caught in a cobweb. Beside them was the bright re
kite that Carlos and Beatrice had bought Luis o
their last trip into Santa Barbara.

When she saw them, she had to bite her lip t
keep from laughing out loud, but her eyes wer
shining like the sapphires in that flashy weddin

ring of hers. "Were you two attacked by a ball of kite string?"

Flynn gave her a disgruntled look, but Luis hurried to explain in a forlorn voice. "We were gonna fly my kite, but the string's all bunched up. We're never gonna get it right."

"Yes, we will," Flynn said, picking through and loosening the knots. "But the next time you put it in the bottom of your closet, maybe you should put it in a box so your cat will stay out of it. After all, since you live way out here on this island, you can't exactly run to a store on the corner and buy more."

"That's what my mom said."

Flynn chuckled and Annie felt her heart melting toward him a little more.

"Here, let me help," she said.

Flynn glanced up curiously. "Taking the day off?"

Annie's smile faltered, and then grew. "Actually, I'm taking the next four days off. James says he can handle things, and I make it a practice to never argue with the Marines."

One corner of his mouth hitched up and he gave her the most carefree grin she'd ever seen from him. "No, you only argue with me. I knew I should have spent time in the military."

"Why bother?" she asked with a saucy toss of her head. "You already know how to be a commander." Unmindful of grass stains to the knees of her white trousers, she crouched beside them and began sorting the knots. "Here, it's better if you start in the middle and loosen it before trying to pull out the string."

"No," Flynn disagreed. "We need to find one end and follow it through the tangle."

She reached for the center of the snarl at the same time that he grabbed one end. The string wrapped around one of her fingers and jerked her arm toward his chest.

Luis burst out laughing. "Do that again," he demanded.

Flynn unwrapped her finger and lifted his eyes toward her. "We can't both be in charge of this, Annie."

She smirked. "Well, you're the knot head, so I'll defer to your superior knowledge."

"You know, you didn't used to be so sassy."

She settled beside him and watched him pick up the end of the string. "I keep telling you, this is the real me."

"Pity," he sighed, but laugh lines crinkled around his eyes.

Annie felt something shift and settle inside her. It was a moment or two before she realized that the feeling was pleasure. The feeling was so new to her since Flynn had come into her life, and she didn't quite trust it. She knew that she wanted it to last, though.

The job took them almost an hour, but with the three of them working together, they managed to untangle the string. Flynn wrapped it around the string holder, which had an attached handle, and tied the free end to the kite. By this time, Luis was wild with excitement, hopping around their feet, demanding that they fly it right away.

"Well, go tell your mom that you're with Annie and me and that we'll be back in a while."

"Okay," Luis shouted and dashed in the back door of the inn.

Flynn looked at Annie and asked, "Where's the best place to fly this thing?"

Annie threw her hand out. "When I was little, I always flew mine off the rocks at the…" Memory returned and her words died away.

"Where?" He frowned slightly as he looked down at her.

Blinking, she looked away. "At the east end of the island."

"We can go somewhere else."

"Sure." She cleared her throat and said it again. "Sure. On the other side of the pine trees."

He turned and looked off in that direction and spoke without looking at her. "You have to face it someday, Annie."

"I know."

"Someday soon."

"I *know*." Chin up, she turned to confront him, expecting to see irritation, or worse, pity, but instead, sympathy simmered in the depths of his green eyes.

With a tiny gasp of distress, she lifted a hand toward him.

Flynn wrapped his fingers around hers and pulled her to him. "This is what we used to do whenever you heard a plane overhead." With his nose, he nuzzled aside the curls that had escaped from her braid and placed his lips next to her ear. "Put your arms around me, Annie, like you used to."

Trembling, her hands stole around his waist, fitting themselves automatically over the hard muscles and hollows of his back. "I don't remember doing this." Her tone was sorrowful.

"It's all right. You can learn it again. Isn't that what we promised ourselves for the next four days?"

"Yes, but..."

He shushed her and the gentle puff of his breath against her ear sent shivers through her. Was this the real Flynn Parker, this tender lover, this considerate gentleman? Was this a side of him that only she had seen? And what kind of woman had she been when she had seen it? She knew what might have attracted her to him in the first place. His solidity, the sense of security that he offered would have been very attractive to her. But what had drawn him to even speak to her in the first place, much less marry her? Once again, she felt regret over what her memory had lost.

"Flynn," she whispered. "I need to know what it was like...what I was like...before."

"Tonight, Annie." His deep voice spoke the assurance into her ear. "We'll talk about it tonight."

His lips feathered over her cheek. Annie quivered with delighted anticipation, wishing he would kiss her fully. She turned her head, intending to take care of the matter herself, when a voice full of disgust spoke up behind them.

"My mom and dad do that all the time," Luis stated flatly.

"Which is how you came to be here," Flynn answered, pulling away and smiling at him.

"Huh?"

Annie stepped away, giggling at the little boy's puzzled expression. She swept her hair from her face, then touched her cheek, still warm from Flynn's kiss. She caught his eye and blushed at the sensual promise she saw there.

Rubbing her hands together, she said in a hearty tone, "So, let's go fly that kite, shall we?"

"That's what I've been wanting to do." Luis reached out to take the kite from Flynn, then he grabbed Annie's hand and began tugging her along. Flynn entwined his fingers with those of her free hand and the three of them headed toward the pine trees.

It was almost noon before they returned to the inn. Luis ran on ahead to tell his parents how high they'd flown the kite. Flynn and Annie dawdled along behind, holding hands as they walked, enjoying the day.

A high-pitched sound in the distance had Annie clenching her fingers against Flynn's and looking toward the sky. "What is that? It doesn't sound like Gary Mendoza's plane, and we're not expecting any guests until tomorrow."

He tightened his grip on her hand. "I don't know, unless..." Just then the plane, a small jet, came into sight.

"What?" Annie asked, wondering at the sudden tension in him.

"It's mine. That jet belongs to the Parker Hotel Corporation."

"Did you send for it?" she asked in confusion. "I thought you were staying."

"I am." He met her eyes. "It's probably my mother and sister."

CHAPTER SEVEN

FLYNN went to meet his family at the plane and bring them up to the house in the Jeep. Annie waited at the top of the entry steps.

She had changed into a blouse and full print skirt, hoping to look mature and yet welcoming.

She felt almost sick with nerves. She had barely reconciled herself to having a husband, much less in-laws. Flynn said she had never met them before, so she would be as much of a surprise to them as they were to her.

Discovering that morning that she had fallen in love with Flynn, quickly and completely, already had her in a state of nervous excitement. The thought of dealing with his mother and sister was enough to make her hyperventilate.

Flynn had said he'd called them that morning and explained the situation and circumstances of her memory loss. She wondered if they would be as initially skeptical as Flynn had been.

Annie heard a step behind her and glanced around to see Mary and James approaching. She smiled at them and hoped it didn't look as fake as it felt. "Taking a break?"

Mary sniffed as she reached out to smooth the collar of Annie's cream silk blouse. "I don't have to spend all of my time in the kitchen," she said. "Occasionally, I do emerge into the light of day."

Annie's laugh stilled some of her nervousness and she reached for Mary's hand.

"Honey," Mary went on, clasping it. "I wish you'd told me about this as soon as he came. I knew something was wrong."

Annie gave her an apologetic look. "I know. I'm sorry, but I was in shock, I didn't know what to do."

"You're married," Mary said, and shook her head. "I know you explained all the circumstances this morning, but still..."

"Imagine how shocked I was when *I* found out."

"Are you going to try and make it work?"

"I...I think so. But it's scary."

Mary gave her a shrewd look. "But not as scary as the idea of walking away from him—or letting him walk away from you."

Annie's lips trembled and she squeezed Mary's hand. "I've always said you know me too well."

"And now you're about to meet his family," James added.

"Yes." Annie swallowed the lump that had formed in her throat. Her lips twitched into a smile as she focused on them. "Why did you say you came out here?"

Mary and James exchanged looks that questioned the stability of her mind. "Because you're about to meet his family," James repeated.

Tears rushed into Annie's eyes. Of course, the two of them were her family, much more so than Uncle Vernon had ever been. "Thank you," she whispered. "I didn't realize how much I needed your support."

When the Jeep came into view, they walked down the steps to meet it. Knowing she wasn't alone helped Annie step forward to greet Catherine and Brenna Parker. During the flurry of introductions that followed, she was able to observe them.

Flynn's mother was petite, with blond hair artfully frosted to camouflage the gray, serious green eyes like his and a watchful expression. Brenna was tall, blond and frankly curious about Annie.

Although Annie felt buoyed by having Mary and James with her, she was conscious of the reserve in the Parkers' manner and felt waves of distrust coming from them. She was grateful when Flynn came to stand beside her and place his arm around her waist. When she glanced up at him, she saw that the look he was giving his family was challenging, and she realized that she had his support, too.

Mary offered to make cold drinks for all of them and bustled off to the kitchen. James returned to the front desk to answer the phone and Flynn took the three women up to his room. James called after them that the phone call was for Flynn.

"I'm expecting a call from Houston," he said, giving his mother and sister a warning look as he walked into the other room. "I'll make it short."

As soon as he was gone, Catherine Parker folded her hands in her lap and gave Annie a direct look. "We're only going to be here for the afternoon. I have a charity committee meeting tonight and Brenna must return to school."

Annie looked from one to the other of them. "I see. Well, it's nice you could come today—"

"This isn't exactly a social call," Brenna interrupted. "We love Flynn, and we don't want you to hurt him again."

Catherine tried to shush her daughter's rash statement, but Annie broke in. "I didn't hurt him deliberately the first time," she said hastily.

"Whatever. The result was the same. He came on this vacation with the express purpose of making a decision about beginning divorce proceedings against you."

"I know that, and now you're concerned because that's not going to happen."

"Unless you do the same thing again, then I hope he'll divorce you and quit trying to hang on to an unreasonable dream." Brenna's tone was aggressive, but Annie didn't take offense because she realized it was prompted by genuine concern for Flynn.

"Maybe it would help if I explained about my amnesia." She gave them a quick rundown of the facts. "I know it sounds like something out of a soap opera," she said apologetically. "Believe me, it's no easier for me to understand than it is for you."

"We're very sorry about the trauma that you experienced over the deaths of your parents," Catherine said. "But we've never heard of this condition before..."

"And we're afraid it'll happen again," Brenna finished for her.

Annie shook her head. "That's not likely. I'm stronger now, and I can face things." She thought of Flynn's insistence that she visit the airstrip and the crash site and hoped she spoke the truth. "You have nothing to fear on his behalf. You see, I love Flynn, and I'll do my best never to hurt him."

The two women studied the sincerity in her face, then looked at each other. Finally, Catherine nodded. "I believe you. I realize that you're as shocked by meeting Flynn again as he was to find you, and that the two of you need time to work things out."

Brenna's face softened and her lips lifted in a hint of a smile. "Don't let him run over you, though, and make all the decisions himself."

Annie held up her hands. "That's another thing you don't have to worry about. I'm catching onto that very quickly."

When Flynn finished his call and hurried into the room, he found the three of them laughing. Annie saw relief flash through his eyes before they settled on her. With a loving smile, she lifted her hand and invited him to sit with her.

Flynn, being Flynn, took it one step further. He joined her on the settee, slipped his arm around her and pulled her against him. Even when Mary brought their cold drinks, he kept Annie beside him and she knew it was his way of declaring that the two of them were together. She could only hope that it was permanent.

Bluesy music drifted from the stereo and out onto the terrace where Annie waited alone. She had the place to herself because most of their guests had departed that day. Catherine and Brenna had left just after dinner. Annie was happy to have met them, and relieved that they seemed to accept her.

Annie closed her eyes briefly, enjoying the evening's quiet. Taking advantage of the lull in business, the other staff members had taken the night off. They were in the lounge, watching a movie from James's extensive video collection. Even the troublesome triplets had joined them.

Flynn had left a message with James saying that he had to make a business call to one of his hotel managers but he would be down soon.

Even though the inn was almost empty, she wasn't worried. A dozen businesspeople and their spouses were coming in for a weekend retreat. They would be using the dining room, the lounge and her family's old apartment for their group meetings. She had been thrilled and surprised when the call had come just that afternoon to make the arrangements.

Since taking over the operation of the inn, she had hoped to book such groups because they often became repeat guests, which could be the lifeblood of a small hotel like hers. It would be good to have the place full for the first time that season. A few more groups like that one, and she wouldn't have to pay the inn's bills according to their urgency, but could pay them when they came due.

She gave a relieved, lighthearted sigh and turned to lean against the railing of the terrace that looked out over the wide lawn. She was wearing the outfit she'd purchased in Seattle, the one she couldn't remember buying. She tucked her hands into the pockets of her skirt, a sweeping circle of ivory silk that had a wide-necked silk pullover sweater to match.

She rubbed her upper arms, although the sweater was enough to ward off the evening chill. She was feeling it more than usual because she was missing the warmth and weight of her hair. Instead of letting it hang down her back, she had swept it up and pinned it into a loose knot, then stood before the mirror in her favorite outfit and worried that she was so obviously dressing up for Flynn. She had never been the type, as a girl or as a woman, to throw herself at a man. But this man was her husband, so surely that made it all right. Along with her acknowledgment of her love for him, she felt a flood of gratitude for the way he had supported her when facing his family.

She had even taken her wedding ring from the safe and slipped it on. Strangely, it seemed to fit better this time and she saw its beauty, the care that had gone into its choosing rather than its size and flashiness. She suspected that if she had it appraised, its worth would take her breath away. She stared down at it, turning her hand so that it flashed and gleamed in the terrace lights.

Other than to call it flashy, what had been her reaction when Flynn had first given it to her? What kind of woman had she been that she could accept such an expensive gift? Perhaps a woman in love? She would find out tonight, she hoped, and begin to understand her reasons for marrying Flynn after such a short courtship. Annie walked the length of the terrace, tracing her hand lightly along the metal railing. If she was honest with herself, she would admit that she already understood how it had happened.

She sorted through her first impressions of Flynn, which were those of anger, heat and power. His claim that he was her husband had shocked and terrified her. And yet, she had felt his shock, too. Later, she had seen his determination to get the answers he sought from her. She had felt overwhelmed by him as if she was caught up in a tornado that was spinning her along.

She had also come to know that he took a hands-on approach to the hotel business, not hesitating to pitch in and help. No matter who he was dealing with, he was smart, resourceful and decisive.

The day they had just spent had shown her another side of him. She placed her palm over her cheek, imagining again the warmth she had known at his touch. He could be tender. The knowledge sent shivers of delight and gratitude through her. She had nothing to fear from him.

Seeing Flynn with Luis and his kite had shown her something else she hadn't expected. The fact that he'd had the patience to spend nearly an hour untangling the kite string had amazed her. She'd never really thought of him in terms of dealing with children. Now she couldn't seem to forget his thoughtfulness with Luis. She closed her eyes and pictured them together, running through the low chaparral bushes, trying and finally succeeding to get the kite airborne.

Frowning, Annie shook her head. The child she kept picturing had her own strawberry-blond hair and Flynn's dark green eyes.

"What are you looking so puzzled about, standing out here all alone?" Flynn asked from the door behind her.

Startled, Annie spun around. He was leaning against the doorjamb, his arms crossed over his chest, his eyes taking a lazy survey of her appearance. His eyes sharpened, then narrowed, and he pushed away from the door.

"Annie," he said, his voice a low murmur as he came toward her. "Why are you wearing that dress?"

She looked at it, and then at him. His back was to the light and she couldn't read what was in his eyes, but his shoulders had gone tense. He reached out to touch the loose weave of her sweater and she thought she saw a fine trembling in his fingers.

"It...it's my favorite. I've had it..."

"More than two years, at least," he said, dropping his hand. "You were wearing it the night we met and you wore it two weeks later when we were married. You wouldn't let me buy you a new one. You said it had to be something of your own."

With a soft oh of surprise, she gathered handfuls of the rich silk as if to hold on to its familiarity while yet another surprise shook her.

"You may not remember, but I think your subconscious does, otherwise why would you have worn it tonight?"

Annie darted him a look from beneath her lashes. "To look pretty for you," she answered honestly.

A deep grumble of satisfaction came from Flynn's throat. "It's about time we started making some progress around here." He took her arm.

"Come on. We're going upstairs to my room where we can have some privacy. Ever since you announced we're married, I've felt like the prize exhibit at the zoo. In spite of our pleasant afternoon with my family, Mary's taken to sharpening knives whenever I appear around the kitchen."

Laughing, she let him tug her along. "You're exaggerating."

"No, I'm not," he insisted. "You should see those blades—sharp enough to do surgery on an armadillo."

They hurried up the stairs together and Annie's excitement grew with every step. Was this how her love for him had felt the first time? This tingling, swirling joy and wonder?

Once they reached his suite, he whirled her inside and closed the door quickly, as if afraid she would change her mind. Annie had no thought of that. She stood with her eyes shining, trying to catch her breath. Glancing around at the cozy room, she noticed that a fire burned low in the grate, sending warmth into the room. It was nothing compared to the heat she felt when she looked at her husband.

Holding her gaze with his, Flynn stepped forward, locked his arms around her waist and drew her to him. He kissed her with slow, lingering passion and increased the pressure until it thrummed through her.

It made her think of the appreciation a man showed for a cup of water after a trek across the desert. She reached up, placing her fingers together at the back of his neck, striving for more.

Annie's heart went wild in her chest when he groaned long and low, as if some terrible, lonely thing was being wrenched from him. Her hands tangled in the thick richness of his midnight hair.

"Annie," he finally said, pulling away. "I promised you some answers. You'll never get them if we keep this up."

With reluctance, Annie settled back on her heels, took a deep breath and opened her eyes to find him smiling at her. It was the happiest she had ever seen him, but she noticed that his breathing was as ragged as hers.

Blushing, she stepped out of his arms and sat down on the chintz-upholstered settee. "All right. So, tell me. Start from when we met at the grand opening of the Heritage Hotel. You were there to see what the competition was up to?"

Flynn gave her a piratical grin. "Hey, they invited me."

"Rather like inviting the fox inside the henhouse, but go on with what you were about to say."

She might have expected him to come and sit beside her, or at least to take the chair across the room, but Flynn paced, as if movement could make the words come more easily. He prowled the room, poked the fire, added another small log and finally settled with his elbow on the mantel and the heel of his short walking boot hooked over the edge of the hearth.

"You were standing by the concierge's desk, answering questions, directing people on tours through the meeting and banquet rooms. You never got ruffled or irritated even though there was a crush of people all demanding your attention."

Annie tried to picture the scene but failed, since she couldn't recall a single detail of the hotel, much less its grand opening. "And I gave you directions?"

The corner of his mouth tilted up. "Yeah, to the men's room."

When she smiled, he said, "It was the only thing I could think of at the moment."

She couldn't imagine him having trouble coming up with an opening conversational gambit. "Go on," she said.

"I came back when the crowd had thinned out. I brought you some punch and some food that I'd swiped off the table reserved for the hotel owners and their guests."

"You have no shame."

"I had to talk to you, get your name, find out about you."

Annie looked at her hands, and then at him. "What did you want to know?"

Flynn walked across the room to stand towering over her. When he answered, his voice was a low, seductive rumble. "Whether or not you were married. It wouldn't have mattered if you'd been engaged, not even if it had been the eve of your wedding. I would have wanted you."

"Why? I have to know . . . I've been desperate to know since that first day in this room. Whatever did you find attractive about me?" She spread her hands wide, palms up. "In that photograph, I look shell-shocked, so sad."

He sat beside her, and before she knew it, she was scooped up and settled onto his lap. His hard thighs cradled her bottom, his arm braced her back, and his right hand reached to hold her hand. He smiled when he saw the ring and brought it to his lips to kiss it. Annie's fingers tightened in his.

"I saw a woman who was like an oasis of calm in the middle of that chaotic opening. You never got ruffled or upset, even when some fat old guy with cigar breath stepped on your toe. You seemed so self-contained, as if nothing could ruffle you."

Annie lifted a brow as she looked at him. "You saw me as a challenge, didn't you? One you couldn't resist?"

"At first," he admitted unrepentantly. "But when I asked you out, and you said yes again and again, I knew I was on to something."

"Did you realize that I was hiding something? That I was emotionally distraught?"

"Yes," he said, slowly. "But I decided that as long as you weren't an axe murderess or a bigamist, I didn't care. I knew, I just knew that if I was patient, you'd tell me everything."

"You had a lot of faith in yourself."

He shook his head. "No, I had a lot of faith in how you seemed to feel about me. You never talked about yourself much, and said nothing about your family or background, but I knew you were trustworthy."

"How could you possibly have known that?"

"You see, Annie, you didn't seem to care about my money, about my family connections or anything else. You didn't talk much, but you listened."

Her lips trembled. "And you figured a woman who listened to you was too good to let get away?"

"Something like that." Flynn reached up and tucked a tendril of fiery hair behind her ear. "And besides, you were so damned beautiful."

With hands that shook, Annie cupped his jaw. "Flynn." She choked, her voice full of the feelings that were overwhelming her. She had a truth for him, too, one that she couldn't keep to herself. "Flynn, I love you. I must have loved you all along. My body has known it since you came to this island, and now my mind does, too."

"Annie." His voice was a thread of sound as he spoke her name and tightened his arms around her.

Her hands on his face, Annie held him off. "Flynn, I don't know what will happen. I don't want to live away from here, but your company, your family..."

"We can work it out," he promised. "We can work anything out now that I have you back again. And now, let me love you. You're my wife and it's been such a long, lonely time."

Annie opened her arms and surrounded him with her love. Flynn covered her mouth with his, holding her in place with his lips and his arms. He stood with her secured against his chest and carried her into the bedroom.

He stood her beside the bed and reached to take the pins from her hair. Within seconds, his deft fingers had loosened her curls, sweeping them down across her back. All the while, he murmured words of appreciation to her, for her looks, her sweetness, the perfection of her body.

When he grasped the hem of her sweater and began to pull it upward, she looked at him with worry in her eyes. "Flynn, I . . . I don't know how to do this," she admitted in a sorrowful tone. "I don't . . ."

"Shh," he quieted her. "You said your body remembers me. Honey, just let it take over."

With a nod, Annie surrendered her worries. Shyly, then with growing boldness, she unbuttoned his shirt, reveling in the dusting of dark hair on his flat stomach. She raked her fingernails through it, drawing a grumble of pleasure from him.

Within moments, they were skin to skin. Annie knew she should have been self-conscious, nervous, shy, but when he drew her onto the bed, she felt nothing but love, excitement and pride.

This was her husband and what they were doing was right.

Annie woke feeling more content than at any other time she could recall in the past two years. She stretched, opened her eyes and took a moment to get her bearings before memories of the night before came flooding back.

She rolled onto her back and smiled at the ceiling, knowing full well that she should be feeling a bit embarrassed, or at least a little shy. What she felt was happiness that bordered on smugness. She turned her head on the pillow and frowned when she realized that her husband wasn't there. She didn't have a lot of experience as a wife, but she knew right away that she didn't like waking up alone.

Raising herself on one elbow, she listened for the shower, but heard only silence from the adjoining bath. Finally, she heard the low rumble of Flynn's voice in the other room. Since his was the only voice she heard, she assumed he was on the phone and lay back to wait for him to return, deciding on the spot that his next vacation—*their* next vacation— would be spent far away from anything even resembling a phone.

She curled up on her side and lay there daydreaming. She felt breathless at the speed with which Flynn had come in and taken over her life.

In less than a week she had gone from being single to being a wife. She now understood how she had fallen in love with Flynn so readily in Seattle, because it had happened again here on her own island. It seemed that some things were destined, some people were fated to be together.

She had never been one to believe strongly in fate. She had especially wanted a concrete explanation for her parents' deaths, but had never found one. And now, what else besides fate could explain the way Flynn had come back into her life? What else could explain the ease with which she had fallen in love with him, just as she had the first time? What else could explain her choice of a man whose life was elsewhere?

Annie began forming possible plans that could keep them on the island and let her husband carry on his work. Her contentment was disturbed by a sudden testiness in Flynn's voice. It rose and fell in a tone she'd never heard before—absolute disgust and anger.

Alarmed, she grabbed his bathrobe, which was on a chair by the bed, shoved her arms into the sleeves and belted it as she stumbled toward the door. She eased it open to see him standing with his back to her. He had pulled on a pair of jeans, but no shoes or shirt, giving Annie a good view of the lean, hard muscles in his back and his wide, flat shoulders. Her fingers seemed to tingle as she recalled touching him. He was leaning on the mantel as he had the night before. This time, though, his manner was urgent, the set of his shoulders tense. As she watched, he paced away from her, stretching the full length of the phone cord out as he walked toward the window. When he spoke, his words were sharp, staccato. She felt sorry for whoever was on the receiving end of his wrath.

"No. Not yet," he said. "She's not ready for that. You'll have to wait . . . Until I think it's time, that's how long . . . Either do as I say or the deal is off. It may be off, anyway."

Even from where she was standing, Annie could hear a squawk of distress. She murmured in surprise. The caller made the very same demanding noises Uncle Vernon made.

Flynn clapped his hand over the mouthpiece and spun around to face her. He looked startled, and then she was amazed to see guilt touch his face.

She blinked rapidly. "Flynn, is something wrong?"

"No." His answer was quick and sharp, and then, as if realizing how he'd sounded, his expression softened, his eyes grew smoky. "Be right with you."

Keeping his gaze fixed on her, he growled into the phone, "I'll talk to you later. No, don't. *I'll* phone *you*. Wait to hear from me."

He hung up while the caller was still protesting. The man seemed to be instantly forgotten as Flynn placed the receiver on its cradle and moved toward Annie.

"I thought you'd sleep longer."

Annie smiled and couldn't conquer the blush that climbed her cheeks. Her blue eyes sparkled as she gave him a shy glance from beneath her lashes. "I woke up and you weren't there."

Flynn took her into his arms and kissed her, long and slow. Sighing happily, she wrapped her arms around him and poured out her heart full of love. Deep in his throat, he made a satisfied sound that she was coming to love, but she felt lingering tenseness in the grip of his hands across her back, tasted urgency in his kiss.

Raising a hand to his cheek, she looked at him with concern. "Flynn, is something wrong? Was that someone from your office? Business?"

"It was business," he confirmed. He cradled her chin in his hand and ran his fingers over her soft skin. "Annie, we need to talk."

"Not yet," she insisted, going up on tiptoe and kissing him again. All her assurance of a few minutes ago fled. She didn't want to be reminded that he had a big company, a chain of hotels to run. Right now, at least for the next few days, she couldn't stand for anything to intrude on their time together.

"Can't it wait?" she asked with a flirtatious smile.

"Annie, it's important." The decisiveness in his voice ended when she tucked her thumbs into his belt loops and began tugging him toward the bedroom.

His breath drew in sharply. "Annie..."

"You were saying?" Her eyes shone with bold mischief.

Flynn swept his hands down, breaking free. He bent and lifted her into his arms. Annie threw her arms around his neck and they kissed all the way to the bed.

"You're sure not the sweet, shy girl I married," he said, opening his arms and letting her fall among the tangled covers.

"Aren't you glad?"

He didn't answer because he was too busy shucking out of his jeans.

"What are you doing?"

Annie popped her head out the door, took a quick peek around and popped into the room. Self-consciously, she tried to smooth a few more wrinkles out of the sweater that had spent the night on the floor. "Looking to see if the coast is clear."

Her husband grinned at her. "It's not like we've been doing anything illegal."

She shrugged and ran her hands over the front of her sweater one more time. It looked awful. *She* looked awful. Her hair was a mess. She had nearly snapped Flynn's small comb in half trying to untangle it. Exasperated, she sifted her fingers through it and let it fall across her back. With her whisker-burned cheeks, kiss-swollen lips and tangled hair, she looked like a wild woman.

"Well, no, nothing illegal, but I'm wearing the same outfit I wore last night. I don't have a speck of makeup on and..."

"It's two o'clock in the afternoon."

She cleared her throat. "Uh, yes, that about sums it up."

Flynn picked up his jacket as he walked toward her. "And you're embarrassed?"

Annie shrugged. "Everyone here knows me so well. They're like my family, especially since... Well, they've never seen me..."

"Spend the night with a man."

"That's right. Nor have I ever..."

"Brought one home?"

She turned her hand up in a helpless little gesture. "That's right."

"I'm damned glad you haven't brought men home, not that there's been much chance of that, living way out here on this island." He held the door and urged her forward.

"I love this island," she began, then stopped, realizing this wasn't the time for such a discussion. She was blissfully happy and wasn't willing to allow cold reality to mar that happiness.

Flynn seemed willing to take her statement at face value. With his hand on the small of her back, he propelled her toward the stairs. "I know you do, but right now, the only thing we'll both love is some food. Why don't I go see if I can find us something to eat—that is, if Mary isn't gunning for me—and ou can change clothes? Put on some jeans. The un's shining, there's no fog. We're going for a walk.''

Before Annie knew it, they were downstairs, he was in the kitchen, sweet-talking Mary, and she was digging through her closet for her snuggest-fitting jeans and favorite scoop-necked T-shirt of emerald green.

As she dressed, braided her hair and put on makeup, she decided that she really was going to have to do something about Flynn's take-charge attitude. A little of it went a long way.

He seemed bent on making decisions for them and on arranging matters to his satisfaction. She wasn't going to let him get away with having things his own way all the time. She would do something about it, too, she thought, rummaging through her dresser, just as soon as she chose the perfume he would like best.

CHAPTER EIGHT

"WHERE are we going?"

"We're going to walk the perimeter of th
island."

Annie rocked to a halt on the top step. She wa
feeling alive and aware, full of the sensory delight
Flynn had awakened in her. She wanted to take th
remainder of this day slowly and savor eac
moment. She did not want to walk the perimete
of the island.

Flynn was three steps down before he realize
she wasn't beside him. He glanced back and caugh
her disgruntled look. "What's the matter? Can'
move? Chewing gum stuck on the bottom of you
shoes?"

"Very funny," she groused, descending the stair
to stand beside him. She threw out her hand in a
arc wide enough to encompass the Pacific. "Do yo
realize it's eight miles around this island?"

"Eight point two, but who's counting?" He in
dicated the supplies he'd hooked to his belt. "That'
why I brought water and sent you back for
sweater. What's the matter? Don't you like t
hike?"

Annie waved her finger about an inch from hi
nose. "I distinctly remember the word 'walk
coming from your mouth. You never said anythin
about hiking."

She thought with dismay of what might happen to her best jeans and the new T-shirt that was a gorgeous shade of green. She'd chosen it especially because she hoped it might complement her eyes. She didn't want it dirtied and stained by perspiration. In the past couple of days she'd discovered a streak of vanity in herself that had never before surfaced.

"A slight oversight on my part," he answered with an unrepentant grin.

She placed her fists against her waist and said, "Now I suppose you're going to tell me that I loved to hike, got up every morning at six to stomp the streets of Seattle."

Flynn tucked his tongue into his cheek and regarded her with devilish intent. "Would you believe me if I did?"

"No. I can't have changed that much!"

"Then I won't bother to lie." He grabbed her hand and started off at a fast clip. "Let's go."

It was either follow or have her arm pulled out of its socket, so Annie followed. Besides, it was fun to walk along hand in hand.

They descended the path to the beach and strolled along the edge of the water, watching as it was displaced by the descending soles of their sneakers. She was grateful for the easy start to their hike. Walking on the water-packed sand was a good warm-up for her leg muscles. Having her hand held securely in Flynn's was a good warm-up for the rest of her.

"I thought we'd take a shortcut across the eastern tip of the island," he mentioned casually a few minutes into their excursion. "Is there one?"

Annie threw him a grateful look. She wouldn't have to face those deadly rocks today, and wouldn't have to make an issue of it, either. He might have self-confidence to the point of being overbearing, but she was thrilled to discover that he also had a sensitive side. It added yet another facet to her love for him.

"Yes, there's a path." The rescuers had used it when they had extricated her parents from the wreck. Annie's mind veered away from that memory. "It goes straight through the chaparral, but it's smooth going."

They started off, Flynn earning her gratitude by maintaining a slow pace and shortening his strides so she could keep up. They wandered along at meandering speed and climbed over rocks where the beach was too narrow to let them pass.

They stood on a windswept bluff. Flynn wrapped his arms around Annie, his chin resting in the brightness of her early-autumn colored hair, and watched sea lions lying on rocks like fat sunbathers soaking up sunlight.

Annie told him about the whales that were visible from November to March as they migrated south to warmer waters, and about the mass of monarch butterflies that had blown in one year. A storm had knocked them off course from their usual migratory route and they had spent several days attached to the island's few trees, turning them into fluttering fantasies, which enchanted her.

On one section of rocky shore where tide pools formed, they picked up sea anemones that twitched and curled at their touch, then set them carefully back in the water.

As they walked and explored, Annie convinced Flynn to talk about himself. She learned about his relationship with his parents, which seemed to be caring and cordial, especially with his late father, but not really warm. It wasn't until he mentioned his sister, Brenna, that he really opened up, proudly telling of her accomplishments in school, her love of animals and her fiery abilities as a jazz piano player.

His description made Annie glad she had met her and eager to know her and Catherine better.

Half an hour after they left the tide pools, they reached Annie's favorite part of the island, a small, private cove warmed by the sun and sheltered from the wind. The inn's employees and guests kept the place busy during the summer season, but today, with few guests in residence and the staff preparing for the incoming businessman's retreat, the cove was deserted.

Or so she thought. "Look," she said, pointing to a pile of articles in a protected corner of rocks. "Someone's left one of the inn's beach blankets down here." It irritated her, since she knew how much they'd cost, especially the monogramming, and she had no desire to replace them because of carelessness.

"I had Carlos bring this down a while ago," Flynn said.

"A picnic on the beach? We just ate." But her protest was only halfhearted. She was already lifting the blanket, handing it to Flynn to spread on the sand, and opening the small basket to find a bottle of wine in a damp clay cooler, fresh grapes and several of Mary's exquisite petit fours.

Sighing happily, Annie took a dainty bite of one, the better to make it last, and then handed one to Flynn. "How did you manage this? Mary only makes these on special occasions."

One of his dark brows lifted as he reached out a hand and motioned for her to sit on the blanket. "Isn't that what this is?"

"I suppose," she answered, giving him a wary look as she crossed her ankles and settled beside him as gracefully as a feather drifting to earth. "Does this special occasion have a name?"

He slipped the wine from its cooler and drew two glasses from the basket. "Reunion?" he suggested. "Belated first and second anniversaries? Missed Christmases? Honeymoon?"

"Didn't we have a honeymoon?" She sipped the wine, savoring it. Had they done this before? Had impromptu picnics on the beach? No. She could answer that for herself. Not in Seattle in February.

"When I suggested it, I learned you wouldn't fly."

"Where did you want to go?"

"San Francisco, to meet my family, then to a cabin the company owns. It's private. Has a view of Mount Tamalpais."

"But the driving time would have taken days."

"Yeah." Flynn filled her wineglass. "And I didn't intend to spend my honeymoon sitting behind the wheel of the car."

Annie blushed, and he grinned.

"That's why I never met your family."

"Right." The look he gave her was quick, tinged with regret. There was absolutely nothing she could do to change the past, but she wished she could. "I didn't push it. Figured there was plenty of time."

She gave him a dry look. "Did you suspect I had other secrets? Like an entire life?"

"Of course, but again, I thought you'd tell me when you were ready. I thought maybe..."

"What?"

Flynn leaned back on his elbow. "I thought you were ashamed of your family, or that they'd been abusive to you."

Annie was shocked by the idea. "No. Never! They weren't just my parents. They were my best friends. Growing up here—" she indicated the sunny cove, the jade-colored sea only yards from their feet "—we were isolated. I had few playmates except for James. When he went away to school, I had no one, so they played with me. I guess you'd say we were unusually close, but it was good, it was nurturing."

"Well, then, don't you think it's about time you faced their deaths?" Flynn asked the question with calm rationale that should have brought a calm answer from her. But the subject wasn't one she could treat calmly.

"I have." Shakily, she set the wineglass down. It tilted, spilling the dark liquid across the light blue blanket. It made her think of blood. Lurching to her feet, she moved away.

"Why are you doing this?" she asked, pushing her hands against her heaving stomach.

"I only asked you a question." He was beside her in an instant, his big, warm hands turning her toward him. She refused to look up, keeping her eyes fixed steadily on the intricate stitches of his navy blue sweater.

"This is a beautiful day, a rare thing this time of year," she said, attempting a laugh that came out in a quaver. "Why spoil it?"

He touched her chin with the edge of his hand, urging her to meet his eyes. Slowly, reluctantly, she complied, but tears were gathering and threatening to spill over.

"Because you haven't really faced it, dealt with the loss."

"I deal with it every day."

"You've never been back to the crash site, or to the airstrip."

"Why would I want to go there?"

"To say goodbye."

"I've done that!"

"You've avoided it." His voice was consistently calm, but the expression in his eyes was relentless. "You can't have a future—*we* can't have a future until you deal with what happened in the past."

"You've been saying that for days," she accused in a tired voice.

"Then you must have figured out that I'm not going to drop this."

Her heart was beating with a heavy thud, so dreadful it shook her whole body. "Flynn, there's something I haven't told you. In fact, I haven't told anybody, not even Mary or James, be- cause...because it hurts so much."

His hands tightened on her arms. She looked at him and saw compassion. "Tell me."

Her breath came out in wheezing gasps because the words were coming up from a deep, dark well where they'd been hidden for years. "When... the accident happened. When...their plane... crashed...my mother didn't die right away."

Flynn's hands tightened reflexively on her arms, but she didn't stop. Now that it was coming, like some horrible malignancy being torn from her body, she didn't want it to stop. She was ready to let it go.

"I ran down to them because I was the only one around. I could hear from behind me that Mary and the others in the inn had heard and would call for help, but I had to reach them."

Flynn didn't prompt her, only waited.

"My father...my father was dead. I knew that right away, but the passenger door of the plane had popped off the side where my mother was sitting...lying." Annie halted, fighting her breath around the nausea that clawed in her throat. "There was blood.... She looked at me and smiled, then lifted her hand. I held it, and she died." Annie pressed the back of her hand to her lips. "It was so quiet."

"Is that all you recall?"

"All that I recall clearly. The rest is just flashes, pieces, until it fades completely."

"Until you found yourself alone in Seattle."

"Yes."

Flynn's fingers swept tears from her lashes and she realized she'd been crying. These tears were healing, though, as he'd said they would be. She should have done it sooner, talked about it and healed herself.

Flynn wrapped his arms around her and held her close. When she stopped crying, he handed her a napkin filched from the picnic basket so she could dry her eyes. Then he gathered her into his arms again and held her. With her ear pressed to his chest, she could hear his heart. It seemed to beat in time with her own. She felt that she was part of him.

At last, he drew away. "Let's go up onto the landing strip. We can start there, walk the length."

She nodded, feeling drained and yet peaceful.

They left the picnic makings to be picked up later and made the ascent from the cove. Fog was drifting in, purling in white eddies on the paved surface of the air strip, blocking out the sun.

They didn't speak as they walked its length, her small hand enclosed securely inside his larger one.

When they reached the end, Annie stood back and surveyed its length. "Somehow it seems smaller than I remember."

"Or maybe it only looms large in your memory."

"Maybe," she murmured and felt a terrible weight shift and free itself from her heart. She still had to go and look at the rocks where the crash had happened, but she didn't have to do it today. This was enough for today. She gave him a smile that was both tired and relieved. "Let's go home, Flynn."

His look was full of pride and, she hoped, love. Though he'd never said it, she was sure she could read it there. Then she saw his eyes darken and shift away from her. "Annie, now there's something *I* need to tell *you*."

Although she didn't like the somber tone in his voice, she nodded with confidence. After all, what could be as bad as the horror she'd just faced?

Before he could speak, they both heard an airplane overhead. Its drone grew louder and louder as it approached through the magnifying fog.

Annie shuddered, but Flynn held her steadily with his arm around her shoulder, and the shaking stopped.

"It must be the group coming in for their business retreat," he said.

"They're not due until tomorrow."

They moved back from the pavement in time to see Gary Mendoza's plane appear out of the fog. It seemed to hang suspended for a moment before dropping down to the small runway and taxiing to a stop.

Gary didn't turn off the engine, which told her he had only a single passenger, with no baggage. When she saw who was stepping from the plane, she groaned in dismay.

"Uncle Vernon," she said, and heard Flynn mutter a fierce curse. She cast her husband a puzzled glance and stepped forward to greet the small, wiry man with the dissatisfied expression and fake smile on his face.

Annie frowned at him. Her uncle rarely smiled and then only if the joke was at someone else's expense. He was dressed in a threadbare suit she'd never seen before, and she wondered if he'd bough it off the markdown rack at a thrift store.

She knew why he was on the island. He'd called frequently to say he needed money. Also, there wa the big surprise he'd mentioned.

She stepped forward to greet him, but he ignored her. In stunned amazement, she watched him wall up to Flynn and hold out his hand. Flynn's fac was about as welcoming as a tropical storm. Hi jaw was set and his eyes were like daggers.

"Hello, Parker," Vernon said in his hearties voice. "You ready to make me an offer on this plac yet?"

Flynn didn't answer Vernon, but turned im mediately to Annie. His hands reached toward he and his eyes demanded that she take them. "I you'll listen, I can explain," he said.

Something in his face had Annie backing awa from him. Her blue eyes were wide and puzzled "What...what's he talking about, Flynn?"

"This was the big change I had in mind, Annie," Vernon broke in, oblivious to the tension betwee his niece and Flynn. "I was going to wait for th right time to tell you, but this is as good a time a any. Parker, here, is considering buying the plac He's been after it for a while, but I told him w couldn't let it go yet. Now's the time, though." H rubbed his hands together in eager anticipation then added as an afterthought, "He'll probably let you stay on as manager, won't you, Parker?"

Annie stared from her uncle to her husband. For an instant, all of her senses seemed to be sharpened. She could hear Gary's plane revving and then shooting down the runway for takeoff. She didn't flinch away from the sound with her usual dread. It wasn't as horrifying as the suspicions that were forming in her mind. She could feel the fog stealing around them, blanketing them with its cold dampness. The scent of the sea filled her nostrils and her mouth, but for some reason, it tasted like bitter ashes.

Why wasn't Flynn saying anything? Why wasn't he denying Vernon's story? Annie kept her eyes on Flynn, waiting for him to tell her that Vernon was lying. He was silent. His eyes were watchful. She couldn't tell what he was thinking.

"I didn't know until you called me this morning that you were here," Vernon rambled on, speaking this time to Flynn. "If I'd known, I'd have been here to show you around personally. Annie runs the place, of course," he said, his tone pompous and dismissive. "But I own the major share of the business, as I told you before, so we can make a deal whenever you're ready."

Flynn's eyes darkened until they were the color of the Pacific just before a storm, his lips drew together, and his jaw tightened. "Shut up, Davidson," he said, barely sparing a glance for the other man, who gaped at him. He stepped toward Annie, but she backed away again.

Her lips trembled so that she could hardly speak
Her momentary numbness was giving way to a tida
wave of emotions—shock, anguish, with betraya
riding the crest. It cut through her as sharply as
sword blade.

When she finally spoke, her voice broke. "Why
Why didn't you tell me?"

Vernon didn't seem to realize that she wasn'
talking to him. Obtuse as always, he went on. "Be
cause you'd have said no and it would have led t
an argument. I've been pretty considerate, yo
know. I waited two years after Christina and Jaso
died before I talked to Parker here about buyin
the place, and since it's not making much mone
anyway, we might as well sell." He turned to Flynn
"Like I told you, I can do that without my niece'
consent. After all..."

Flynn cut a look at Vernon that would have slice
through steel. His voice was low and lethal an
came through his teeth like the menacing growl c
a wolf. "Davidson, I said *shut up.*"

Vernon's eyes bulged and his Adam's appl
bobbled in his scrawny throat. "Sure, sure, Parke
whatever you say."

Dismissing him, Flynn turned to Annie. "W
need to talk."

"It's a little late for that, isn't it?" she aske
her voice hitting a high note of hysteria. Her han
came up to her throat as if to hold her heart i
place.

Vernon frowned at the two of them, but whe
he started to speak, Flynn quieted him with anoth

look and held out his hand to Annie. "Let me explain," he said.

Annie shook her head as her slim body began to tremble. She wrapped her arms around herself as she continued moving backward, away from Flynn. She couldn't tear her eyes from his face. It had gone cold, stiff. She saw a flicker of some emotion, disappointment or despair, as if he hadn't expected this reaction from her.

She almost laughed. What else could he expect? She opened her mouth to speak, but the words wouldn't come. Finally, she shook her head at him, turned and fled.

Behind her, she heard Vernon ask, "Why do you think you owe her an explanation?"

"Because she's my wife, you insensitive jerk. Now get out of my way so I can catch up with her."

Vernon's squeak of surprise and Flynn's furious voice calling her name followed Annie as she ran, disappearing into the fog that was lying low on the island.

She considered running to the inn, hiding in her room, but if she saw Mary or James, they would question her, and she couldn't face them right now. Her breath cut through her lungs from exertion and panic as she ran. Finally, she reached the cliffs and the path leading down to the private cove. The heavy dampening mist made the descent slippery, but Annie barely noticed as she scrambled to the sand. The picnic items were where she and Flynn had left them.

She stumbled to a stop, staring at them. They seemed an obscene reminder of the happiness she had felt only minutes before. With a sob, she collapsed on the blanket and pulled it around her. The pain of Flynn's betrayal twisted in her, and her mind kept replaying every moment with him, every look, touch and gesture that had made her love him. She had been such a fool.

She cried until her tears were exhausted, then she rubbed her eyes dry with her knuckles and huddled on the beach, staring dry-eyed at the ocean as the waves crested and broke.

Why had they done this without telling her? She had a right to know about anything that affected her livelihood and that of her employees. Of course it was no secret why Vernon had tried to sell the inn. He needed money. He always needed money. He was a bottomless pit for money. He was also selfish and shortsighted.

But why hadn't Flynn been honest with her? Why hadn't he immediately told her the real reason for his presence at the inn? Vacation, indeed! He was there to examine the property he hoped to add to his hotel chain. If it was a vacation, it was certainly a working one.

Several things made sense now, and each one added to her disillusionment.

Flynn had asked many questions about the workings of the inn. He had probably volunteered to cook when Mary was sick just so he could get a good look at the kitchen equipment and supplies they had on hand. No doubt, it wasn't up to Parker Hotel standards and he intended to upgrade it.

He'd even known the exact perimeter of the island. Probably had some office flunky look it up.

Flynn had also known the inn was in financial trouble and losing money because her blabbermouth uncle had told him all about it. Vernon was such an inept businessman he didn't know that if he wanted to sell, he was supposed to play up the island's good points and not just concentrate on pointing out its faults. He didn't have any business knowledge, sense of family loyalty or even common sense. Annie only tolerated him because he was her mother's brother, the only family she had left.

Her sense of betrayal began to fade, and fury took its place. Flynn Parker had a great deal to answer for. Annie knew his surprise at seeing her was genuine. His reaction wasn't one that could have been faked. But once he knew who she was, that she was his misplaced wife, why hadn't he told her about his negotiations with Vernon?

He was her husband, and while he hadn't bowled her over with declarations of love, he had insisted that their marriage was a real one.

She sat up suddenly and stared unseeing at the ocean while her mind made several connections concerning their marriage. She had just answered her own question. Flynn didn't want her. He didn't love her. He only wanted the inn and the island. All the signs had been there, but she'd been too overwhelmed by him to see them.

It was horrible, rotten, and she wouldn't sit by her huddle on the beach another minute and let them get away with it.

Annie jumped to her feet, gathered the picnic items and hurried to the foot of the path, only to realize that the tide was coming in. The way to the

path was blocked by slowly rising water. The on
way up was to scale the face of the thirty-foot blu
It was either that or spend a freezing night on t
beach.

Clicking her tongue in exasperation, Ann
stowed the basket and blanket on a high ledge o
of reach of the water. She would send Martin
Carlos down tomorrow to retrieve it.

Standing back, she studied the cliff. All the w
around the cove, the first seven feet of the cliff h
been smoothed by high tides and storms. The or
way out was narrow and steep, but offered plen
of handholds. She'd climbed it before, but it h
been years before, and her father had been wi
her, acting as her climbing partner. Now she h
only herself to depend on.

She snorted derisively as she pushed up the sleev
of her sweater and rubbed her hands together
warm them. She might as well get used to c
pending only on herself. Once she confronted Fly
and Vernon and told them the inn wasn't going
be sold, she knew she'd be alone for a long tim

CHAPTER NINE

ANNIE studied a handhold that was two feet above her head, but it led to several more that would get her out of this predicament. Backing up several feet, she made a running dash toward the cliff and leaped for the handhold, but fell short.

Backtracking, she was ready to try again when she heard a voice shouting from overhead.

"What the *hell* do you think you're doing down there?" Flynn yelled.

Annie threw her head back and spied him standing at the top of the cliff. "I'm having a picnic and I didn't invite you."

"I've been looking all over for you."

"You found me. Now leave."

"Not until you come out of there."

Even with the fog eddying around him and obscuring his features, she could tell by the wide-apart set of his feet and the hands clamped to his waist that he was absolutely furious. She couldn't have cared less so she lifted her voice and matched him shout for shout. "I'm *trying* to get out of here."

"What happened? Did you sulk so long you let the incoming tide catch up with you?"

Annie's hands clenched into fists. "I wasn't sulking."

"Wait there," he commanded as he looked around, gauging her situation. "I'll get a rope."

"I don't need a rope, and I especially don't need your help, Flynn Parker."

"Well, you're going to get it, *Mrs Parker*," he roared. "Don't move."

He disappeared and Annie ignored his order. With a toss of her head, she backed up, then took off running and leaping once again—and falling short once again.

Furious, she kept this up, failing each time until the high tide began coming in earnest and her feet were soaked. After half an hour, she slumped against the side of the bluff and fought for breath.

A few minutes later, she heard the roar of the Jeep's motor, then the sound was abruptly cut off, followed by running steps.

"I told you not to move," Flynn shouted from over her head. "You're going to exhaust yourself."

That had already happened, but she'd be darned before she would admit it. She straightened away from the rocky wall and glared up at Flynn, who was snaking the end of a thick rope down the face of the cliff. It galled her to accept help from him, but she reasoned that it wouldn't lessen the impact of the things she intended to say to him as soon as she reached the top.

"Tie the end around your waist," he shouted. "And I'll pull you up."

"Tie the end around a rock or the winch on the Jeep," she yelled back. "And I'll pull myself up. I don't need your help."

"You're being stupid and stubborn."

"Thank you, I cherish the compliment."

When there was no response, she grabbed the rope, tied it snugly around her waist, then braced her feet against the rock face and started up. She hadn't taken three steps before the muscles in her arms began to burn. The ones in her legs quivered and her knees felt weak. She took another step, gasping with the effort, knowing she wasn't going to make it out of there on her own.

Then she felt the rope tighten and she was being pulled inexorably upward. By holding on tight and bracing her legs, she managed to keep herself from scraping against the rocks. In less than a minute, she neared the top and could see Flynn with one end of the rope wrapped around a rock, then around himself, hauling her up, hand over hand.

Feeling awkward and at a disadvantage, she scrambled onto the top of the cliff, untied the rope and threw it in his direction. Without bothering to thank him, she turned to stomp down the path to the inn.

"Wait a minute," Flynn shouted, tossing down the rope and striding after her. He caught her arm and spun her around to face him.

The color in her cheeks was high, her eyes were livid, and her hair was a wild tangle around her face. She was breathing hard, her blood already up, spoiling for a fight.

He was ready to provide it. He gestured toward the cliff. "That was a stupid thing to do."

"Not as stupid as trusting you."

"I didn't know your uncle was going to show up today."

She clapped her hands onto her hips. When she spoke, she wagged her head furiously from side to side and her tone was sarcastic. "Well I didn't know you were planning to buy my business, *my home,* right out from under me."

"I admit that I came here for my vacation because I was interested in buying the place. The Parker Hotels board wants us to start a division of small inns, bed and breakfast places, hostels..."

"Oh, and you're their front man? Going out ahead like a scouting party, tricking people out of their property?" With a sneer, she turned away, but once again, he brought her back. This time, though, he held her in place, his hand manacling her arm. His face loomed closer and her chin came up another notch.

"I've listened to the last accusation I'm going to hear from you." He shook her arm lightly, but she could feel the strength in his hand. He was holding himself firmly in check. His hard breathing matched hers, and his eyes were as stormy as the incoming tide. "Now, you're going to hear everything I have to say and you're going to think about it."

"So talk." She wanted to sound uncaring, but her voice cracked because she was deeply hurt.

"Vernon contacted my office several weeks ago, saying the inn was for sale. He'd picked up information through the grapevine that my company was searching for properties. I agreed to look the place over and let him know. He said his niece, Anne, ran the inn and would be opposed to the sale, but he was the owner. I didn't tell him exactly when I'd be here, because I knew he'd be all over, trying to sell me the place. When I came here, I had no idea that my long-lost wife was the niece he'd been talking about.''

"But once you found out, why didn't you tell me?" She held up her hands. "Never mind. I've already figured out the answer to that one. I've heard you're a ruthless man, but this is a new low, even for you."

His jaw jutted forward as he glared at her. "What are you talking about?"

"I'm talking about the way you deceived me. You don't want me. You want this inn. Telling me to face the past and deal with it, that we could work out the past and the future—those things were lies."

Flynn's hands shot out to grab her and pull her against him. "I've never lied to you, and I never will. You can always believe what I say, and believe this, too." He covered her mouth with his, kissing her until he had stolen every bit of her breath. He jerked his mouth away and ground his forehead against hers. "Does that feel like I don't want you?" He pulled her lower body against his. "Or this? Listen to me, Annie. I could buy any inn on the west coast. I don't have to have this one. Think about that."

He released her suddenly and she stumbled away from him. Childishly, she rubbed the back of her hand across her lips, trying to scrub away the taste of him, but it was useless.

"I still don't understand why you didn't tell me."

Flynn sighed. "Because once I saw how much you loved this place, I decided to proceed slowly."

She led with her chin. "Now that you know, and you know that I'll never agree to the sale, why don't you just proceed right off this island?"

"Why do you want to keep struggling to make this inn pay?"

She clapped her hand against her forehead. "Haven't you heard a word I've said? Because this is my home, my business. Everything that's important to me is here."

Challenge bloomed in his eyes. "Everything, Annie?"

"Yes." Why did that feel like a lie when she said it? She refused to acknowledge that he was important to her. It hurt too much.

He stepped closer and his voice was a purr. "The last I heard, you loved me, Annie."

"It's not the first foolish thing I've said." She didn't want to show weakness before him, but she desperately wished she could press her hands against her chest. She felt that her heart was breaking up into little pieces. She'd heard that clichéd phrase many times before, but she'd never known a person could actually feel it happening.

Flynn's voice softened. "It wasn't foolish."

"You won't hear it from me again. The last thing you'll hear is, 'I'm filing for divorce.'"

"Like hell." Flynn raked his hands through his hair and the dark strands clung together, damp from the fog. "Look, this inn needs repairs and upgrading and you can't afford to do that without an investor."

"You mentioned that before, but I didn't realize you were seeing yourself in that role."

"Why don't you just hear me out?"

She waved a hand at him. "By all means, proceed."

"If I don't buy the inn, or at least invest in it, your dear uncle will sell it to someone else."

Annie looked at him with horror dawning in her eyes. She hadn't thought of that.

"Better the devil you know than the one you don't know, wouldn't you say?"

Overwhelmed by her uncle's treachery, she couldn't answer.

Flynn placed his hands on her shoulders and turned her toward the Jeep. "Go on, get in," he insisted. "I'll drive you back. You can rest for a while, take a shower. I'll come get you for dinner. We'll talk to your uncle together."

"No, thanks, I'll walk back to the building, and I'll talk to Vernon myself. He's my uncle."

"And I'm your husband."

Annie's shoulders slumped. She couldn't fight anymore. This day had been too full of emotional shocks. She was worn out. She wanted to go to her room and shut the door, not see anyone for a while until she had resolved what she should do. She especially didn't want to see Flynn or Vernon.

"I have to do this myself, Flynn."

"No, you don't. You have a partner now, whether you want one or not. You don't have to do everything yourself."

Without answering, she turned away. She was several yards down the path when something compelled her to look back.

Flynn had returned for the rope and was busy looping it in his hands. He was watching her. His eyes were thoughtful and his expression was as bleak as her own.

"What's *he* doing here?"

Annie didn't even have to look across the dining room from the windowed kitchen door to see who James was talking about. He only used that tone of voice when her uncle showed up.

"Does he need money?"

She nodded. "Of course he does."

"I guessed as much. That's the only reason he ever comes here." James gave her a sharp look. "You're not going to give him any, are you?"

"Not on your life."

"Good. I don't think Flynn would let you, anyway."

"This has nothing to do with Flynn," she snapped, but when James's eyes widened, she smiled weakly. "Sorry, I'm on edge."

James answered with a faint smile of his own. "Like it or not, Annie girl, everything in your life has something to do with Flynn Parker now."

That was becoming abundantly clear, but she wasn't ready to acknowledge it out loud. "I didn't expect Vernon to come. I don't like having him around."

Vernon was seated alone at a table. He looked out of place there, a solitary, unhappy man drinking his way through a bottle of their best white wine. Across the room, Mabel, Mavis and Mildred were laughing and talking about their day's excursion.

into Santa Barbara. They had visited a hairdresser and were delightedly comparing hair color, now three interesting shades of blond. A young couple sat in one corner, engrossed in each other and ignoring Mary's luscious dinner. Witnessing their happiness made Annie wince, and she looked back to her uncle.

She was going to have to talk to him and she wanted to do it before Flynn came down, so she might as well get it over with.

She received a sympathetic look from James as she walked across the room and took the seat across from Vernon. He barely glanced up.

"Vernon," she began, "I know we've never really gotten along, especially since Mom and Dad died."

He gave her a black look. "You don't like me, and I think you're a goody two shoes."

It was a struggle, but she decided to ignore that. "I don't think you understand the financial situation here."

"You're losing money."

"Unlike you, it's through no fault of my own," she said icily. "We had a bad winter, but things are picking up. Legally, you have a right to share in the profits of the inn, but you've never really given me a chance to try to make things work."

"You've had two years."

"Two years of learning," she admitted. "I'm just now finding my way, learning everything I need to know..."

"Why bother?" he asked, taking another swallow from his glass. "You don't need to now. You've got a rich husband to buy into this place. He can throw away as much money as he wants."

"This has nothing to do with Flynn." She sat forward and leaned across the table. "Don't you see? You're trying to sell our family home—"

"One I've always hated."

There was no denying that. He'd proved it over and over throughout his life. Annie kept a firm rein on her temper as she tried to think of another approach. The idea of selling the inn was so foreign to her that she found it hard to understand his motive. She knew what it was—personal gain—but she couldn't understand it.

"Tell me about your marriage to Parker. How come I didn't know about it? How come I wasn't even invited to the wedding?"

Taken aback, Annie sat up straight. She should have realized he would ask, but she wasn't going to give him an answer. She had never told him about her memory loss because she had discovered long ago that for Vernon, information was power, and she didn't want him to have any power over her. It was bad enough having him involved in the inn.

When she didn't answer, Vernon went on. "How come he didn't say anything about it when we started negotiating for this place? Was he going behind your back?"

A hot denial shot to her lips, but she swallowed it down. How could she deny what she was thinking herself? Sharp feelings of betrayal warred with her love for Flynn. She stood suddenly. "I don't think it's going to do any good for us to talk about this," she said, and walked away.

She called herself every kind of a coward as she hurried across the room, and then started calling herself a hypocrite. She couldn't answer Vernon because she had no answers for herself.

In agitation, she ran her hands down her moss-green skirt, aware once again of their tenderness. Even though she had balked at taking orders from Flynn, she'd done as he had said, showering and resting for a while before dinner. She had discovered several scrapes on her hands from the rope she'd used to climb the cliff. Funny, she hadn't noticed them at the time, but she'd been too incensed at Flynn to pay much attention to anything but him.

As furious as she wanted to be with him, she wondered why he hadn't come to get her for dinner. As hurt as she was by his deception, she had begun to think about what he had said. Vernon was determined to sell, if not to Flynn, then surely to someone else. One way or another, she was going to lose the inn, her heritage. At least if Flynn bought it, some arrangements might be worked out so that she could manage it. Over and above her worries about the inn, she needed to work out her feelings for Flynn. She loved him. She had admitted it to herself, and to him, despite her denial in the heat of anger. She needed to talk to him, to get everything out in the open.

Annie hurried to the kitchen where Mary and Beatrice were cleaning up. Quickly, she prepared a tray for Flynn, carried it upstairs and knocked softly on the door. It brought back memories of his first day at the inn. Had that been less than a week ago?

When he called out, she entered, balancing the tray on her hip. The room was dark, the only light coming from a flickering fire laid in the small fireplace. Flynn was stretched out on the settee, one foot thrown over the arm, the other resting on the floor. His head was tucked awkwardly into the corner formed by the arm and the back, but he lay motionless as if unaffected by the uncomfortable position. He didn't acknowledge her as she walked in.

Annie set the tray on an end table. "I've brought you some food."

He tilted his head and looked at her through narrowed eyes. "Not the actions of a woman bent on divorce, Annie. You're sending me mixed signals, here."

She ignored that. "I...I noticed you didn't come down to dinner."

"Oh, yes, and you were worried because I'd promised you we'd talk." He rose to his feet and ambled across the room. He took a chicken leg from the plate and began munching on it as he leaned against the mantel. "So, did you talk to Vernon?"

"I tried, but not for long."

"Have trouble communicating?"

"The only language he listens to is money."

"I've got money."

"I know. That's what this is all about, isn't it?"

"Are you ready to listen now, be rational?"

With a resigned sigh, she nodded and moved to sit in a chair. Flynn turned on a light and when he faced her, she could see he was as tense and strained as she was.

"What's your worst fear about this situation, Annie?"

"Losing..." To her surprise, she almost said, "you." Her gaze shot up to meet his. Indeed, that was her greatest fear, but she hadn't known it until this moment.

"The inn?" He misinterpreted her and she was too shaken to correct him. "How could that happen? California is a community property state. Half of this business is yours, and half will still be yours if I buy Vernon out."

"I hadn't thought of that," she said faintly.

"That's because you're reacting with your heart instead of your business sense." His eyes were keen. Even in the dim light, she felt that he was looking right through her. "You don't want to leave the island."

"No."

"Do you think this is an enchanted place, like Brigadoon or the Land of Oz? Are you afraid you'll never get back if you leave?"

"No, of course not. Don't be ridiculous."

Flynn tossed the chicken leg on the plate and came to stand before her. "You dread leaving."

"So?" She dreaded it almost as much as she dreaded losing him—and yet, he hadn't been honest with her.

"Do you dread leaving here or dread facing up to your responsibilities?"

"I always face up to my responsibilities."

"Oh, really? What about your marriage?"

He had her there, and they both knew it. She could walk away from him. After all, she wasn't the same woman he had married, and in so many vital ways, he was still a stranger to her. But she loved him.

"How do you suggest I face up to them?"

The tension in his arms went slack, as if he'd been braced for a battle and his opponent had surprised him. "I suggest you leave the inn in James's care for a while and come to San Francisco with me. I have a business to run, and in spite of what you think, it will be good for you to get away from here for a while."

She stared at him. "I . . . I can't leave the island now, with the big group that's coming in. I'll be needed."

Flynn's jaw clenched. "And it doesn't matter if I need you?"

She wasn't sure he ever needed anyone, but she couldn't think of any way to answer him. She needed him, there was no doubt of that, but she also needed to know where this marriage was going. So far it was a marriage of smoke and mirrors. It had been built on mystery and the withholding of truth. And yet she loved him. There had to be a way for them to resolve the past and establish the future. She didn't know how to put that into words, though. And if his true motive was ownership of the inn, she didn't want to risk rejection.

While she struggled for an answer, Flynn turned away. "I guess silence is as good an answer as any," he said, picking up another piece of chicken. "Thanks for the dinner, but you didn't have to bother. It's a little too much of a wifely thing to do. Not quite in character for you."

"Now wait a minute," she flared. "I'm not the one who arrived here with a secret agenda. I've told you everything I can recall, and . . ."

"Forget it, Annie. Why don't you go see if there's anyone or anything else on this island needing your attention? I'd say you've given me about as much as you can for today."

Stung by his unfairness, Annie rose and walked to the door. She looked over her shoulder at him, a welter of emotions filling her heart.

His face was weary and drawn, roughened by the beginnings of a five o'clock shadow. He met her eyes with a flicker of pain.

Annie told herself that he was the one who was in the wrong. So why did she feel guilty?

"Annie?"

"Yes?"

"I'm going to meet with your uncle tomorrow morning at ten. Since it involves the inn, you might want to be here."

Annie frowned at him. "I just talked to him. He didn't mention it."

Flynn raised an eyebrow at her. "He doesn't know yet. Don't worry, for once in his life, he'll be responsible and show up. After all, I'm the man with the money. He'll want to hear what I have to say."

"Are you going to do it?" she demanded. "Are you going to buy him out?"

He crossed his arms over his chest. "I've learned one thing in this business, Annie, and that's, don't tell anyone what you're going to do until you've done it."

"Even your wife?"

He started walking toward her. "Seems to me we've come full circle in this conversation. The rights of a wife—or a husband—include the responsibilities. Are you saying you're ready to face up to those, too?"

She had no answer for that, and he knew it.

He snorted. "As the old movie serials used to say, 'Stay tuned for the next episode.'"

"I'll do that," she said, opening the door and sweeping out. "I'll just do that." Even if she hadn't known what an inadequate response that was, his answering laugh would have told her.

CHAPTER TEN

ANNIE rushed down the stairs and across the entry-way, then came to a stumbling stop. She felt angry and restless, wanting to take her frustrations out on work, as she had for the past two years. Right now, there was little to be done. There were few guests and they all seemed to be occupied with one activity or another. A pile of bills waited on her desk, but she couldn't pay them any more now than she could have when she'd left them there yesterday. Besides, she wasn't sure she could settle to a task, no matter how much it needed to be done.

She turned and rested her back against the arched entryway, looking at the chandelier that hung suspended from the ceiling. It sent a soft glow of light across the white-painted surface but was thankfully too dim to illuminate the many cracks that were beginning to show in the white plaster. If she had the money, she could have the ceiling fixed.

She could buy new nets for the tennis court, golf carts for the golf course, update plumbing and furnishings. There were dozens of things she could do if she had the money.

If Flynn bought out Vernon's share in the inn, she would have what this building needed—money not only for repairs, but for mundane things like paying bills and meeting the payroll. It was true that money wasn't everything, but she had employees to consider.

If Flynn invested in the inn, she could stop worrying and enjoy being an innkeeper—but what of being a wife? It seemed obvious that keeping the inn meant she wouldn't be living with Flynn. And living with him in San Francisco meant she wouldn't be here to run the inn.

Restlessly, she moved away from the wall. She couldn't allow herself to think of Flynn as a way out of her financial troubles. She still felt betrayed by him.

That wasn't all that bothered her. She loved him in spite of everything, but their marriage was too shaky to withstand the pressure of distrust between them. He wanted to invest in the inn, and she certainly needed a backer, but throwing money at the problem wouldn't solve it.

If the other things could be worked out, she wanted him to know that she loved him for himself. But there was another side to that coin. She wanted to be loved for herself, too, not because she possessed a piece of property he wanted, or because she had disappeared and he'd found her again. She still didn't know if he wanted their marriage to last because of who she was now or who she'd been when he married her. And she wouldn't have any answers until tomorrow, if then.

Annie wandered from the room, automatically checking the dining room and kitchen as she went through, looking for anything that was out of place. Everything was neat and tidy, telling her that the staff could carry on just fine without her. They could handle things with no problems if she went to San Francisco.

She grimaced. There was no *if* about it. Flynn had said he wanted her to go with him, and she knew him well enough to know he wouldn't take no for an answer. If they went, they would only be transferring their problems, not solving them.

Annie entered her room and moved about straightening the items on her dresser. Her hand fell on a perfume atomizer and she lifted it to her nose. The bottle had been her mother's. The scent was her favorite, a combination of roses and spice.

She had accepted their deaths, and with Flynn's help, she had even begun to accept the way they had died. How could she think she could ever again be separated from a man like that? Shaking her head at the confusing tangle of emotions, she turned away, catching sight of her bed and remembering the night before, spent in Flynn's arms.

Tonight would be a long and lonely one. Resolutely, she picked up a book and settled into a chair. She would read until she was exhausted, and then maybe she could sleep. After that, the challenge would be to keep from dreaming.

The next morning, Annie helped Mary in the kitchen and assisted Beatrice in preparing rooms for the incoming guests. She called their grocery supplier in Santa Barbara and ordered food to be picked up later that day when Carlos took the cabin cruiser in. She brushed her hair, slipped on a simple leather hairband, then smoothed the creases from her apron-style denim jumper. Satisfied, she then went upstairs to Flynn's room to watch her uncle sell her birthright.

On the landing of the second floor, she met Mavis, Mabel and Mildred. They were dressed for golf and all three still sported adhesive bandages on various parts of their bodies from their tennis game two days before.

Annie had always thought of golf as a rather tame sport, but she'd seen the sisters play. She might as well put in a call to the paramedics right now.

Mavis put her hand on Annie's arm and gave it a squeeze. "I must say, this has been the most exciting vacation we've had here in years. Sister's Week has turned out to be a real treat, even if I did have to actually bring my sisters."

The other two women sniffed indignantly, but Annie smiled. "I'm glad you've enjoyed yourself."

"Yes, sir, having Flynn Parker here has been a delightful treat."

"What's Flynn got to do with—?"

"Although I'm furious with you for not telling me Catherine Parker was coming," Mildred added, indignantly shoving her sister aside and nearly toppling her down the stairs. "You let me go merrily off to play tennis and didn't even tell me she was coming here."

Annie's dark blue eyes were puzzled. "She arrived by jet, Mrs Bennett. That's a little hard to miss."

Mildred patted her new hairdo. "I was involved in my game."

"I see," Annie murmured, and bit her lip to keep from smiling. Doubtless, she'd been on the verge of defeating one of her sisters—and if the number of bandages was an indication, possibly even drawing blood.

"I would have loved to chat with her."

"Oh, come off it, Millie," Mabel snorted. "She probably doesn't even know you."

"She does, too," Mildred insisted. "We're quite good friends."

Annie watched in amusement as the two of them continued down the stairs, arguing loudly, leaving Mavis behind. "As I was saying before I was so rudely interrupted by my sisters, having Mr Parker here has kept things lively."

Annie wasn't sure where this was leading, but she admitted to herself that she rarely knew where a conversation with one of the triplets was leading. "Yes, he is a good dancer—"

"Oh, honey," Mavis trilled. "That's only a fraction of it. He's a sexy hunk of man and you're darned lucky to have him, but I'm talking about the way he's made things happen around here." She nudged Annie in the ribs and winked at her. "Not to mention the way he's made things happen around you. You've looked more alive in the past week than you have in the past two years."

Annie's smile trembled. She'd *felt* more alive.

"Yes, sir, that man'll keep your tootsies warm at night. When will you be moving?"

Dismayed, Annie stared at her. She and her sisters had asked the same question once before, and last night Flynn had made it plain that he expected her to go to San Francisco with him. "I don't know," she said. "There's this inn to run, and it's always been my home."

Mavis wrinkled her nose at Annie. "Yeah, honey, this is a great place, but it's just a building. It's not like it's family or anything." She looked over the railing and gave a little squeak of alarm. "Oh, I've got to go or those two will be out on the course before me. Can't have that."

Annie stared after her as she tripped down the stairs, then turned slowly and continued toward Flynn's room. She knocked, then glanced up the hallway to see Vernon shuffling toward her.

He looked the worse for wear. His eyes were bloodshot, his expression sullen. His suit was wrinkled as if he'd slept in it. She wondered briefly if he'd spent the remainder of last evening drinking too much, then decided it probably didn't matter. He would soon be gone, and with enough money to ensure he could drink and gamble to his heart's content. She felt a wave of sorrow that they had never been close, even after her mother's death, but it was tempered by the relief of knowing that if Flynn bought Vernon's share of the inn, she wouldn't have to give him money ever again.

"You're looking smug this morning," Vernon said with a sneer. "I suppose you've been up with the chickens, working to make this place pay. Well, you won't have to worry about that much longer, will you? Your husband can afford to dump money into this place if he wants to. I'll be glad to be out of it."

"Vernon, you were never in it," she sighed.

"Maybe not, but it's about time I got my fair share. You don't know what it's like, always having to beg for what's rightfully mine and..." He started when the door was abruptly flung open.

Flynn glared at Vernon. He was a formidable man at any time, but with his jaw set and his eyes flashing with anger, he verged on frightening. The effect wasn't lost on Vernon, whose mottled face blanched.

"Davidson, if you want to talk business, why don't you come on in and we'll talk business? Otherwise, quit feeling sorry for yourself and trying to intimidate Annie. She won't stand for it, and neither will I."

Annie's eyes widened and she stared at him as a slow realization spread through her. Flynn was on her side. In spite of the obstacles that stood between them, he was on her side.

She wasn't alone anymore. She didn't have to run the inn, or her life, or anything else by herself anymore. She didn't have to struggle over bills or worry over repairs. She had a partner to help her.

Was it possible that the greatest obstacle between them was her own stubbornness? She wasn't the same shell-shocked woman who had returned to the island two years ago and made it her haven away from the world. Now she had to look at herself and wonder if it was a haven or a self-built prison.

She had held on to her pain all this time, never truly dealing with her parents' deaths until Flynn came and forced her to. Even if she didn't love him, that would have been enough to gain her gratitude.

When she didn't follow her uncle inside, Flynn asked sharply, "Annie, is something wrong? Did he say anything to upset you?"

"No." The word came out on a breath of sound and she cleared her throat. "No."

He gave her a concerned look, but stepped back so she and Vernon could enter.

Flynn had spread papers out on the coffee table between the settees. He indicated that Annie and Vernon should be seated opposite him, but Annie came to stand beside him, instead. Her shoulder barely reached to the middle of his bicep, but her message was unmistakable—they were in this together, for better or worse.

Flynn's eyes darted to her, full of surprise that flashed to warmth. The corner of his mouth lifted in a promising smile. When he looked at Vernon though, his tone was cool.

"Davidson, I've decided that I will buy your share of the inn."

Vernon wiggled his head in a triumphant little swagger and gave Annie an I-told-you-so look. "How much?" he asked, sitting up straight. Annie wondered if he expected to have to bargain and haggle over the price, because his face was takin on the same expression he'd had the few times he'd possessed nerve enough to ask her for money in person.

Flynn nodded, as if this was what he had expected. He named a figure that brought a gleam of greed to Vernon's eyes and made Annie's jaw drop. It was more than the full worth of the inn.

"Flynn," she protested. "That's far too much—"

He gave her a sharp glance and cut her off. "As part of the agreement of sale, you're going to promise to never again bother Annie for money."

Vernon stood abruptly as he sputtered out a protest. "Hey, wait a minute, I may need more later."

Flynn crossed his arms over his chest and stared the older man down. "No promise, no sale. No other terms. Take it or leave it."

Vernon stared at Flynn for a moment, then at Annie. The hardness in his expression softened for a moment, and she thought she saw a flicker of the uncle she'd always wished he'd be, one who was capable of selfless love. Then it was gone. He looked away and gave Flynn a nod of agreement as he held out his hand.

"I'll take it. I'll be glad to be rid of this place."

Flynn shook Vernon's hand, then dropped it quickly. "You'll be hearing from my attorney. I want to complete this purchase as soon as possible."

"Good. That's what I want, too." He turned to Annie, who took a hopeful step forward, but all he said was, "Can you get Martin or Carlos to take me to Santa Barbara in the cruiser? I've got things to do."

She swallowed her disappointment and blinked back threatening tears. "Sure, Vernon. Carlos is going in today. I'll call downstairs and have James tell him to wait for you."

"I'll do it," Flynn said. Moving to the phone, he quickly made the arrangements.

"Fine. That's just fine." Vernon rubbed his palms together in anticipation, then walked toward the door. Annie followed him.

She held out her hand, then dropped it helplessly to her side as she tried to think of a way to say goodbye to him. "Vernon, I know you want to be rid of this place, but it will always be your home. You're welcome to visit anytime as long as you abide by our terms."

His reddened eyes widened in surprise and he gave her a weak smile. "Yeah, maybe I'll do that. You don't have to worry about me asking for money again, though. I've got plenty now. It'll last me the rest of my life." He opened the door and swaggered out.

When the door closed behind him, Annie's shoulders rounded in disappointment, then she straightened. It was done. Now she had to deal only with Flynn.

She buried her hands deep in the pockets of her denim jumper and turned to him. "Why are you paying him so much more than his share is worth?

One of Flynn's dark eyebrows rose. "So he'll leave you alone—leave *us* alone."

"You do realize that all that money will be gone in a year?"

"If it lasts that long."

Annie gave him a perturbed look as she crossed the room. "And then what?"

"He'll probably come visit us and ask for money."

"And then what?"

A smile tilted Flynn's lips. "Why, then I'll give him a job and make him earn it, but he'll never again have a claim on you, or on this inn."

"I...I know it's best," she said, hesitantly. "But he's my only living relative, and..."

"You've been responsible for him for too long. He's a grown man. He's got to sink or swim on his own. Besides, he may be your only relative, but he's not your only family. There's Mary and James, Tom and Brenna—and you have me, Annie."

His voice had gone deep and solemn. In his serious eyes, she saw pain and deep regret.

Her lips trembled when she answered him. "I know."

He said in a rush, "Annie, you've got to believe me. I didn't try to deceive you. I didn't tell you about my interest in buying the inn because there was already enough tension between us and I didn't want to muddy the waters."

"I know." She was standing before him now, looking into his face. "You were trying to do what was best for me—for both of us."

He reached for her hand and she felt a small tremor in his fingers. "Yes, I was. I'm glad you understand that."

Her lips trembled when she smiled. "I understand something else, too. I suspect that you intend to give me Vernon's share of the inn and that my name alone will be on the deed."

His chin drew back in surprise. "Well, yes. How did you know?"

She gave him a teasing glance from beneath her lashes. "When a woman's been married as long as I have, she gets to know her husband pretty well. Even if she doesn't remember but one week of that marriage. I was upset and angry yesterday, and shocked. I reacted selfishly and I'm sorry."

"No," he said, reaching to draw her into his arms. His arms slipped around her waist. With his hands clasped behind her, he drew her close. "I'm sorry. It would have been best if I'd told you right away. Brenna tells me I'm too sure of myself and convinced that I know what's right for everybody."

"It's true," Annie admitted.

Flynn's lips tightened for a second. "Annie, I'm afraid I can't change."

"I don't want you to. That's why I love you. You've made me face the worst things that have ever happened in my life and deal with them

Annie put her hands around his neck and pulled his face down to hers. "I have to thank you."

Their lips touched then held. Annie felt love flooding through her. She loved him, and she promised herself that she would spend the rest of her life showing him how much.

When he pulled away, his voice was raw. "Annie, stay with me. Don't let this, or anything, end it for us. I love you. I almost died when you left me before. I can't live through it again."

Annie's lips formed a soft O of surprise. "I . . . I didn't know. You never said," she stammered.

He drew back and frowned at her. "Didn't know? You're kidding. I carried your picture around with me for two years. I carry the pocketknife you gave me. I ran after every woman with hair like yours, thinking it was you. I never even considered filing for divorce because I hoped you'd come back to me. I loved you from the first minute I saw you and I never stopped."

Annie touched shaking fingers to his cheek. "You have to say it sometimes, Flynn. I need to hear you say it."

"I love you, Annie."

"I love you, too, Flynn, and I'm ready to go to San Francisco with you whenever you say."

His lips tilted in a grin. "You must love me if you're willing to leave here, but I'm not asking you to leave permanently."

"What do you mean?"

"I'm moving the corporate offices to Santa Barbara. We can live here and I'll commute."

She swallowed a nervous lump. "By plane?"

"Yes. Think you can handle it?"

She loved him for the anxiety in his eyes. "Yes, I can handle it. You've taught me I can handle almost anything—except losing you through my own stupidity."

He kissed her again, then placed his lips against her ear and said, "Don't ever leave me, Annie. I don't ever want to feel that way again, as if my insides had been ripped out."

Annie kissed him and looped her arms around his neck. "That won't happen. Those bad times are behind us—or almost."

His eyes searched her face. "What's wrong?"

Annie drew a shaky breath. "Come outside with me, please."

"Outside?"

She nodded. "To the east end of the island. There's something I have to do."

He drew his breath in sharply. "Are you sure?"

Her stomach seemed to be bouncing around somewhere inside her rib cage, but she nodded gamely. "I'm sure. Let's go."

He took her hand and they hurried down the two flights of stairs, found the keys to the Jeep and drove to the place Annie had avoided for so long. The path dipped and turned before it reached the rocks.

Annie put a shaky hand on Flynn's arm. Seeming to sense what she wanted, he pulled to a stop a few hundred feet from a small drop-off. Below them were the rocks she dreaded.

Flynn helped her from the Jeep and held her hand as they walked to the edge and looked over.

Annie entwined her fingers tightly with his and held on as she gazed down. She sighed in relief when she saw that there wasn't a trace of the wreck.

Flynn didn't speak for several minutes, allowing her emotions to stabilize. Finally, he said, "I talked to James about this. He said that after the wreck was cleared away and you'd left for Seattle, he and Mary came and picked up every scrap of metal and piece of glass they could find. It's completely clean, Annie. All that's left is the terrible memory."

"Yes," she said, sadly.

"But we could make it into a better one if we built a memorial here."

"What kind?"

He looked out at the jade-green water. "Maybe a chapel. I'll bet there are couples who would love to be married in such a setting." He smiled at her as he drew her into his arms. "In fact, I think we should be the first ones to use it and get married again. That way, you'll have one to remember."

Her breath caught in her throat. "Oh, Flynn, that would be wonderful. I love you for thinking of it." She pulled him down for another kiss.

"My pleasure, Mrs Parker," he murmured, covering her lips with his.

With happiness shining in her eyes, Annie pulled away and began tugging him toward the Jeep. "Come on, husband. We've got things to do if we're going to move your headquarters, build a chapel here and make the inn pay for itself."

"I'm coming," he said, catching her hand and leading the way with his long strides. "In fact, I'm way ahead of you."

Laughing, they ran all the way to the Jeep.

* * * * *

Friday's child is loving and giving...
Look out next month for Ruth Jean Dale's
A Simple Texas Wedding, the latest book in
our exciting series.

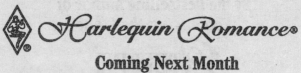

Coming Next Month

#3423 MARRYING THE BOSS! Leigh Michaels
All Keir Saunders was interested in was making money, and so when he needed a wife to complete a business deal, it seemed easiest to buy one! His secretary, Jessica, was the logical candidate. And though she was certain matrimony wasn't in her job description—how could she refuse a man like Keir?

#3424 A SIMPLE TEXAS WEDDING Ruth Jean Dale
It began simply enough when Trace Morgan hired Hope to organize his sister's engagement party.... But Trace didn't want the wedding to go ahead. And he certainly didn't want to fall in love with the hired help!

#3425 REBEL IN DISGUISE Lucy Gordon
Holding Out for a Hero
Jane was a cool, calm and collected bank manager. Gil Wakeham was a rebel. But Jane had accepted his offer of adventure—a summer spent with Gil and his adorable basset hound, Perry. The dog had stolen her sandwiches. Was Gil about to steal her heart?

#3426 SOMETHING OLD, SOMETHING NEW Catherine Leigh
Hitched!
Lily Alexander's husband, Saige, had been missing—presumed dead—for seven long years when he walked back into her life! And though Lily was overjoyed to see him, the timing was awkward, to say the least. Lily's wedding to her new fiancé was imminent! But Lily could hardly marry placid lawyer Randall when her sexy rancher husband refused to let her go!

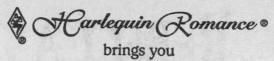

Harlequin Romance ®

brings you

HOLDING
HER◉
OUT FOR A

Some men are worth waiting for!

Every month for a whole year Harlequin Romance
will be bringing you some of the world's most eligible
men in our special **Holding Out for a Hero**
miniseries. They're handsome, they're charming but,
best of all, they're single! Twelve lucky women are
about to discover that finding Mr. Right is not a
problem—it's holding on to him!

In September watch for:

#3425 REBEL IN DISGUISE
by Lucy Gordon

Available wherever Harlequin books are sold.

REBECCA

43 LIGHT STREET

YORK

FACE TO FACE

Bestselling author Rebecca York returns to "43 Light Street" for an original story of past secrets, deadly deceptions—and the most intimate betrayal.

She woke in a hospital—with amnesia...and with child. According to her rescuer, whose striking face is the last image she remembers, she's Justine Hollingsworth. But nothing about her life seems to fit, except for the baby inside her and Mike Lancer's arms around her. Consumed by forbidden passion and racked by nameless fear, she must discover if she is Justine...or the victim of some mind game. Her life—and her unborn child's—depends on it....

Don't miss *Face To Face*—Available in October, wherever Harlequin books are sold.

HARLEQUIN ®

®

43FTF

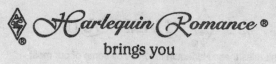

Harlequin Romance ®

brings you

How the West was Wooed!

We've rounded up twelve of our most popular authors, and the result is a whole year of romance, Western style. Every month we'll be bringing you a spirited, independent woman whose heart is about to be lassoed by a rugged, handsome, one-hundred-percent cowboy! Watch for...

- September: #3426 *SOMETHING OLD, SOMETHING NEW*—
  Catherine Leigh

- October: #3428 *WYOMING WEDDING*—
  Barbara McMahon

- November: #3432 *THE COWBOY WANTS A WIFE*—
  Susan Fox

- December: #3437 *A CHRISTMAS WEDDING*—
  Jeanne Allan

Available wherever Harlequin books are sold.

Look us up on-line at: http://www.romance.net

HARLEQUIN®

Don't miss these Harlequin favorites by some of our most distinguished authors!
And now, you can receive a discount by ordering two or more titles!